"What am I  Sophie

"I'd say the same ... babies for hundreds of years. Take her home and raise her."

"I'm a bull rider. I'm on the road almost fifty percent of the time. I'm living in a house that isn't even livable."

Bull rider. That reminder had Sophie stepping back in her car, away from him, away from the tug on her heart and back into her shell. "Yes, well, I'd say you'd better get it livable."

"You could help me."

"I did. I changed the nastiest diaper in the history of diapers." She glanced at her watch. "I'm late."

"We have to talk about the land."

"Later."

"Dinner?" He leaned in, holding tight to Lucy.

"Nope. I don't date bull riders." She started her car and reached to close the door. He stood there, not moving.

"I'm not asking you out."

Ouch. That hurt a little, for some crazy reason. "Good, I'm not accepting."

"Fine, I'll see you later," he said with a grin.

Books by Brenda Minton

Love Inspired

Trusting Him
His Little Cowgirl
A Cowboy's Heart
The Cowboy Next Door
Rekindled Hearts
Blessings of the Season
  "The Christmas Letter"
Jenna's Cowboy Hero
The Cowboy's Courtship
The Cowboy's Sweetheart
Thanksgiving Groom
The Cowboy's Family
The Cowboy's Homecoming
Christmas Gifts
  *"Her Christmas Cowboy"
The Cowboy's Holiday Blessing
The Bull Rider's Baby

*Cooper Creek

BRENDA MINTON

started creating stories to entertain herself during hour-long rides on the school bus. In high school, she wrote romance novels to entertain her friends. The dream grew and so did her aspirations to become an author. She started with notebooks, handwritten manuscripts and characters that refused to go away until their stories were told. Eventually she put away the pen and paper and got down to business with the computer. The journey took a few years, with some encouragement and rejection along the way—as well as a lot of stubbornness on her part. In 2006, her dream to write for Love Inspired Books came true. Brenda lives in the rural Ozarks with her husband, three kids and an abundance of cats and dogs. She enjoys a chaotic life that she wouldn't trade for anything—except, on occasion, a beach house in Texas. You can stop by and visit at her website, www.brendaminton.net.

The Bull Rider's Baby
Brenda Minton

Love Inspired

Recycling programs
for this product may
not exist in your area.

 LOVE INSPIRED BOOKS

ISBN-13: 978-0-373-81621-7

THE BULL RIDER'S BABY

Copyright © 2012 by Brenda Minton

www.LoveInspiredBooks.com

Printed in U.S.A.

A man's heart plans his way,
But the Lord directs his steps.
—*Proverbs* 16:9

I would like to dedicate this book to my agent,
now retired, Janet Benrey. Thank you
for long years of hard work, hand-holding,
encouragement and the careful prodding
that kept me going and kept me focused.
You're more than an agent, you're a friend.

And Melissa, my amazing editor and encourager.
Thank you for everything you do!

To my awesome BFFs, you are always there for me.
I love you and wish we could have coffee every
morning—in person, not on the phone.

And Mary…for being a mom and so much more.
Thank you for making this easier.

Chapter One

When Keeton West entered Convenience Counts store at seven in the morning, Sophie Cooper was the last person he expected to see. But there she was, running down the sidewalk, brushing a hand through her shoulder-length auburn hair. Not really auburn, though. Her hair had always been dark brown. The hint of red probably came from a bottle, but he liked it.

He even kind of liked her in a slim-fitting business suit, her high heels clicking on the floor as she walked through the door. She looked like an executive from some Tulsa high-rise office building, not the daughter of a wealthy rancher. She was a sleek and shiny European car in a world of pickup trucks.

He grinned at that comparison and watched as she hurried through the glass door at the front of the store. He thought about approaching her, and then reconsidered. Exhaustion must be getting to him or it wouldn't have crossed his mind.

For the past two nights he'd gotten almost no sleep. And then this morning he'd gotten up early to head into Dawson for a few necessities. The baby in his arms had insisted on the supplies.

The problem was, he didn't know what things a baby required. She cried, that's about all he knew. And he knew in baby talk, crying meant something. Either she was hungry, needed changing or something else was wrong. At about two in the morning he started to think the last choice might be the correct one. After he gave her the last bottle he had, he was at a loss. A few hours later he found himself here, hiding from Sophie Cooper before he could ask the store's proprietor for baby advice.

"Hey, Sophie, what has you out so early in the morning?" Trish Cramer leaned over the counter at the front of the store. She and her husband, Jimmy, had owned Convenience Counts for as long as Keeton could remember. And they'd always liked to keep tabs on what was happening in Dawson, Oklahoma.

There wasn't a local paper, but the folks in Dawson had Jimmy and Trish.

"I'm just here to grab some breakfast." Sophie grinned at them. She had a smile that could knock a guy to the ground.

She'd always been beautiful. The woman was even better than the girl she'd been years ago. If things had been different, she would have married his brother, been his sister-in-law. If everything hadn't changed on a June night sixteen years ago, that is. But it had changed. Nothing could undo that night.

Keeton sighed and moved around the corner of the shelves he'd been standing in front of, out of the line of sight so that he wouldn't be the first thing Sophie saw when she turned his way.

He peeked, though. Like a thirteen-year-old kid spying on cheerleaders when they'd stopped for a diet cola after practice. Yeah, he'd been that kid. And Trish had given him the eye then, the way she was now.

"You're working on a Saturday?" Trish looked over the tops of her glasses.

"Do you need gas pumped?" Jimmy came around the corner of the counter, wiping his hands on a rag.

"No, I filled up last night. I just need to grab breakfast and go." She stopped in front of the warming tray and eyed food that had been sitting under a heat lamp probably since the place opened an hour ago.

Breakfast pizza and a few egg sandwiches. He'd grab something for himself, once he figured out what a three-month-old baby ate for breakfast. He looked down at the mysterious creature cuddled up against him. For once the baby wasn't crying.

He had to stop thinking of her as "the baby." She was *his* baby. Lucy. She cuddled into him, trusting, even after just a couple of days of knowing him. His baby. He shook his head, the way he'd been doing since his ex-wife had dropped Lucy with him. A baby hadn't been on his list of things to get.

But he had her, and he couldn't imagine not having her. Although he could imagine getting a little more rest. He hoped sleep didn't turn out to be a thing of the past.

"Honey, you're always in a hurry." Trish had moved closer to Sophie. "When are you going to settle down?"

"No time for settling down, Trish. Work keeps me busy."

Trish laughed at that. "Well, that isn't going to keep you warm when the winters are long. You need a husband."

Keeton nearly groaned because when Trish said "husband" she shot him a look over Sophie's right shoulder. He shushed the baby and repositioned her. Babies were heavy. He hadn't realized how heavy a twelve-pound bit of fluff and spit-up could be until he'd spent a full day hauling one around.

"I think I'll be fine. I've got a good furnace." Sophie answered Trish on the husband issue. "I'll just grab something off the shelf."

"All of this hurrying isn't good for your digestion," Trish called out, the all-knowing voice of reason and common sense.

"Then I'll take a pack of those antacids you have behind the counter to go with whatever I buy."

Keeton pulled his hat down low and grinned at the comeback. One thing about Sophie Cooper, she wasn't a wallflower. She'd slapped him once, years ago. He shook his head and reached for a jar of baby food because maybe Lucy needed more than bottles. When he got to the register, he'd ask Trish.

Click click of heels. He watched out of the corner of his eye as Sophie hurried in his direction. With a single step he moved back to the end of the aisle. She stopped in front of the few breakfast items on the shelves, frowning as she surveyed the options.

The baby in his arms whimpered. He bounced her a little, hoping to quiet her down. It had worked last night. He'd spent about an hour swaying back and forth in his living room, wishing he had real furniture and maybe the smarts to tackle his situation a little differently.

Smart would have been not marrying Becka

Janson because he felt sorry for her. She'd played him good. She'd found out his winnings, his earnings and how much he'd invested in Jeremy Hightree's custom motorcycle business and she'd latched on quick. At least he'd been smart enough for a prenup.

The baby in his arms wiggled, squirmed and let out a real cry. Sophie Cooper turned, her hazel eyes widened as she zeroed in on him and the baby. A smile trembled on her lips and her gaze shifted from the baby to him.

He tipped his hat and grinned, knowing charm and good looks weren't going to mean a thing to the woman standing in front of him. Her attention wasn't on him anyway. She looked at the baby, the coolness in her eyes softening, warming.

Man, she hadn't changed much at all. She could still stop a guy in his tracks and make him forget what he wanted to say.

"Keeton West." Her voice shook a little. "And a baby."

He held the baby with one arm and cupped the two jars of food in his free hand. He knew his shirt had spit-up smeared on the shoulder and he hadn't shaved in three days. He couldn't think of a thing to say that wouldn't sound ridiculous.

"Me and a baby." Stupid. Pre-Lucy he would have winked and said something like "It's been a long time." Or, "Sophie, you're as beautiful as ever."

Instead he jabbered like the infant in his arms and echoed her like a fifteen-year-old with his first crush. Actually, he knew fifteen-year-old boys who would have done better.

If he'd had any sense at all he would have stayed in Broken Arrow. He had a nice little place on the edge of the city. But wanting his family land back—that had been his driving force for as long as he could remember. He needed to remember that was his reason for being here.

One thing stood between him and the biggest portion of that land. Sophie Cooper. She'd bought one hundred acres of land that used to be his family farm.

She smiled at the baby, not at him. "She's beautiful."

Next time Sophie would listen to that little voice that told her to run in and get a breakfast sandwich from the Mad Cow. But no, she'd been in a hurry and thought the local convenience store would be quicker.

Surprise, nothing was ever quick in Dawson. Or easy. People always managed to get in her business. If it wasn't her family it was one of the locals trying to find out what she'd been up to, or trying to find a way to marry her off.

Today the problem happened to be Keeton West.

She had one hour to get to a meeting in Grove and then she had her other project to work on. And Keeton West had something dripping down the front of his shirt, very close to where it was unbuttoned at the throat. Very close to the silver cross and chain that he wore around his very tan neck.

She cleared her throat and stumbled back to the present. The main thing she didn't want to discuss with him was land she'd recently bought.

The baby in his arms forced her to act, though. Maybe it had to do with being a Cooper. Or maybe she couldn't run from biology. Even if she didn't have children of her own. Was it her imagination or did she hear a very loud clock ticktocking in her ear?

The baby spit up again.

"Keeton, she's sick." Sophie grabbed a role of paper towels off the shelf and ripped them open. "Here, sweetie. Oh, that's awful stuff."

Keeton West and a baby. She tried to connect dots and couldn't. She couldn't imagine him with a child. And yet... She wiped the baby's chin. The infant had his nose. She had his brother Kade's nose. The thought ached deep down inside Sophie, in a place that had been broken and empty for a long time. It was the part of her heart that still missed Kade. Or what they might have had.

Pudgy baby arms reached for her and big eyes overflowed with tears that trickled down the little girl's pink cheeks. Keeton held tight and Sophie put on a smile that said none of this hurt, none of it mattered. She had survived. She'd gotten past the pain of losing Kade. She was whole.

"Thank you." Keeton's voice was low and husky, his eyes sought hers. And she couldn't look at him, not without seeing Kade. The resemblance shook her. The dark hair. The lean, suntanned features. The dark eyes that danced with laughter or smoldered with emotion. Ugh, she was so not able to deal with this.

When she looked at Keeton she remembered the night he pulled the bull rope for Kade. It was just one of the memories they shared. Common ground that she didn't want to be on today.

"You're welcome." She stood there with a handful of smelly paper towels and nowhere to run to. "What are you doing back in town?"

"I'm here to get our land back."

Oh. Well, she didn't quite know what to say to that. "I didn't know you had a baby."

He grinned, and the ornery leaked back into his brown eyes.

"Yeah, neither did I until a few days ago. Long story but I divorced her mother about a year ago. Or her mother divorced me. And we didn't see each other again until she showed up on my doorstep with what she called a 'surprise.'"

"And where's her mother?"

"On her way to South America with a bull rider she met a few months ago."

"I'm sorry." What else could she say? "What's her name?"

"Lucy Monroe West." He smiled down at the little girl. "And I don't have a clue what I'm supposed to do with her."

"You do what you're doing. Hold her. Feed her. Love her."

"And what do I feed her?" He shrugged a little and looked from Sophie to the baby. "I mean, food? Milk?"

"Formula." Sophie reached for a box. "She's little, Keeton. No food. Not yet."

"Right, formula in a bottle." He juggled the baby and the stuff he'd picked up, putting baby food back on the shelf.

Sophie wanted to take the baby. And she *didn't* want to take her. She couldn't get involved, not with Keeton. That would be a mistake. It would be stepping back into the past. She was thirty-five. She didn't have time for the past.

She had a present to worry about. Her life today filled with too many matchmakers, not enough single men, work and her own projects. Life.

"I should go."

"Right, and maybe we can catch up later."

He smiled when he said it, because he didn't mean it. Neither of them wanted to get together, to relive, to catch up.

"Well, it was good seeing you again." She smiled and moved to slide past him.

"Yeah, it was." He stepped back, the baby in one arm, a teddy bear diaper bag slung over the other and a loaf of bread balancing on top of the package of diapers he had managed to pick up.

The baby watched her, tears in watery blue eyes. For years Sophie had lied to herself. She tried to convince herself that growing up a Cooper, with a dozen siblings and an array of foster children in the home, she could live without babies. She'd had enough.

And it wasn't true. She wanted a baby of her own. She wanted to hold the baby in Keeton West's arms.

She grabbed a cola from the cooler section. Next to her, Keeton jostled the baby in his arms and nearly lost his hold on her.

Instinct took over. Sophie reached, the baby grabbed. Suddenly Sophie had the spit-up-covered baby in her arms and Keeton moved the diapers to his free hand.

"Don't get too comfortable. You have to take her back," Sophie warned. But the baby held tight to her shirt and whimpered. Sophie kissed the little forehead.

Keeton grinned. "But she looks perfect in your arms. Look at the red in her hair. You're a match."

"This isn't…"

He winked then. "Yeah, I know it isn't."

She looked down at the tiny creature in her arms. Lucy smelled positively awful. And she was wet clean through. "You could have warned me."

She held the baby out to him and he looked perplexed. And he looked as if he'd just rode in off the range with his faded Levis, washed-out blue, button-up shirt and dusty boots. Surprise, surprise, he didn't have on chaps, or a gun in a holster on his belt. That would have been a little too Old West, even for Keeton.

"Sorry." He didn't look it. "Do me a favor, hold her for a second. Just give me a chance to get this to the counter."

"You know I will."

She spotted toaster pastries with blueberry

filling and knew exactly what she'd be having for breakfast. With the baby in one hand she grabbed the box and tried to pretend she wasn't a grown woman buying breakfast food that came in a box and contained more sugar than most cookies.

"On a health-food kick?" Keeton grabbed a container of baby wipes. "Let me pay and I'll take her back."

"Why is it I think you'd hit that door running if I gave you half a chance?" Sophie followed him to the cash register and almost parked herself between him and the door. "I go first."

She put her breakfast on the counter and with her free hand dug in her purse for cash. Keeton dumped his groceries next to hers. He also took the roll of paper towels, and the used ones still wadded up in her hands. Those he tossed behind the counter into a waste basket.

"I'm buying." He grinned. "I always told you I'd take you to dinner someday. Looks like I'm buying your breakfast today."

"You really don't have to."

"I owe you." He nodded at the front of her jacket, now soaked and with a trail of spit-up down the front.

The baby turned into her shoulder and started crying. She rubbed her face back and forth on

Sophie's collar. Baby slime. And goo. And she didn't have time to go home and change.

"Keeton West, you never answered." Trish grinned at the infant. "Where'd you get that pretty baby?"

He grinned, and Sophie applauded his silence. If he said anything it would be all over town by the end of the day. Or by lunch.

Trish came around the counter, maternal and an obvious choice to hold the squalling infant clinging to Sophie's collar.

"It's a long story." Keeton dug his wallet out of his pocket and tossed a couple of bills on the counter.

"Well, we've got time for long stories, don't we, Jimmy?" Trish touched the baby's back. "My goodness, she stinks."

"Yeah, I ran out of diapers."

Warmth spread down Sophie's front before Trish could take the baby. Now it wasn't just the back of the baby's sleeper that was soaked.

"Uh-oh." Keeton grabbed the bags Jimmy had set on the counter. "Guess she's wetter than I thought."

"Is she yours?" Trish wouldn't let go.

Sophie handed the baby over to Trish, who obviously didn't care if the infant soaked her clothes. Now that her hands were free, she reached into Keeton's groceries and pulled out her toaster pastries and the can of soda.

"These are mine." Sophie pointed to the baby. "That's yours."

"Is she yours?" Trish pushed on, leaning to kiss the baby's cheek. "My goodness, she's warm. Do you have anything to give her for this fever?"

"Sick and wet, my lucky day." Sophie headed for the door. "Have fun, Keeton."

Keeton, carrying the baby girl and his bag of groceries, caught up with her as she got into her car.

"Wait."

She sighed and stuck the key in the ignition. "What?"

"I want to talk to you about our land."

"*Our* land?" She knew exactly what he meant, but she didn't have time for this. Besides that, she had plans for that land.

"You know what I mean, Sophie. You bought the one hundred that joins up with the twenty I bought. A corporation bought the land on the other side of the road."

"So you're here to buy back West land?"

"That's why I'm here. That farm meant everything to my granddad, even to my dad, before…"

Yeah, before. She looked away, thought about

hollow expressions, loss, giving up. The Wests had sold out to the Parkers, and then the Parkers had split the land up, sold it and moved to Kansas last year.

"Soph, I want to buy it back."

"Keeton, I don't have time to talk."

He leaned in, holding the baby that still hadn't been changed. She cuddled against his shoulder, crying as he tried to continue the conversation. "We need to talk."

The stench of the messy, wet baby proved to be more than Sophie could take. She shook her head and moved to get out of the car. Keeton backed up, his words drifting off as she reached for the baby. "We have to change her before we continue this conversation."

"I can manage."

She took the baby from him and placed her on the backseat of the car. "Give me a diaper. And you'd better have plenty of wipes. And hand sanitizer." She gagged a little just thinking about what was waiting for her.

Keeton handed her a diaper and wipes. And then he had the nerve to step back. She tossed him a meaningful look over her shoulder. "Get back here. I'm not doing this alone. You never send a man, or woman, in alone."

"Right." She heard him take a deep breath and he stepped close.

The diaper was every bit as bad as she imagined. Worse even. After taking it off and cleaning the baby with wipes, she handed Keeton the offending item. He gasped as she shoved it into his hand.

"Don't think you get out of this completely." She smiled over her shoulder at him before turning her attention back to the task at hand.

Keeton took another deep breath and hurried toward the trash. Sophie smiled at the baby. Lucy, blue-eyed and beautiful, smiled back. Sophie lost her heart. And it had been a long time since she'd done that. So long, in fact, she almost expected it to hurt. The heart was, after all, a muscle. She figured hers might be close to atrophy from lack of use.

But she wasn't about to admit that to anyone. She also wouldn't admit that she'd been telling God about her loneliness, thinking maybe He could show her a glimpse of His plan.

"Thanks." Keeton grabbed a few wipes as she taped a new diaper in place. "For your hands. It's the best I can do."

She took the wipes and handed him the clean baby. *Clean* wasn't really the best word. She needed a bath. Badly.

"I'd take her home and bathe her if I were you."

Keeton looked down at his little girl. "Bathe her?"

"Yes, with water and soap. It's a funny little custom most people enjoy daily."

"Not funny. I don't know how to bathe a baby."

"You'll figure it out. And you should run into Grove and get medicine for her fever. Maybe take her to urgent care. She does feel warm."

"Great, a sick baby."

"Probably just a virus. She'll be fine. So will you." She smiled at the sight of him holding the baby. "Daddy."

"Daddy." He looked down at his daughter, his expression downright wistful and a little confused. "I have a kid."

"Looks that way."

And then wistful disappeared, replaced by a look of total shock. "What am I going to do with her?"

"I'd say the same thing parents have done with babies for hundreds of years. Take her home and raise her."

"I'm a bull rider. I'm on the road almost half my life. I'm living in a crash pad, not a home."

Bull rider. That reminder had her getting back in her car, away from him, away from the tug on her heart and back into her shell. "Yes, well, I'd say you'd better make some improvements."

"You could help me."

"I did. I changed the nastiest diaper in the history of diapers."

"Seriously, Soph, I need help."

He sighed and her resolve to be strong, to not get involved, got a little weak in the knees. Not for Keeton, but the baby. "I'll be around if you have a problem. I live in the old stone house, just a half mile from you."

"Right, thanks. And don't think I've forgotten the land. We need to talk."

"Later." She had slid behind the wheel of her car and now she glanced at her watch. She hated being late. She had five minutes to get to Grove for a meeting with a contractor.

"Dinner?" He leaned in, holding tight to Lucy.

"Nope. I don't date bull riders." She started her car and reached to close the door. He stood there, not moving as she'd given the indication he should do.

"I'm not asking you out. I meant we could talk business over dinner."

Ouch. That hurt a little for some crazy reason. "Good to know, but I'm not accepting."

"Fine, I'll see you later. But we are going to talk about my land."

"My land." She backed out of the parking space. She had her own land. It wasn't Cooper land. She'd saved money left in a trust from her grandparents. She'd saved residual income from her allotted fifty acres and the few oil wells still pumping. She had her own space in the world. Her own land.

Her own life that no one else was involved in. Unfortunately her land used to be West land. What had seemed like a great idea months ago now felt like a giant headache about to happen. Or heartache.

After years of being gone, she hadn't expected Keeton to suddenly show up back in Dawson.

As she pulled out of the parking lot she glanced in the direction of Keeton's truck. He stood next to it, strapping Lucy into an infant seat. Seeing her glance his way, he waved and then turned toward Lucy.

Kade's brother. A bull rider. The last person she wanted in her life.

Chapter Two

Keeton lugged the infant car seat into the ramshackle house that he now called home. It had electricity, running water and little else to recommend it. The porch sagged in places and a few boards were missing. The living room was long and narrow with only two windows and floors that creaked when he walked across them. He put the baby down on the sofa he'd hauled in a few days ago.

She had fallen asleep halfway home, after sucking down a bottle, burping loudly and then fussing with hiccups for a few minutes. If she'd stay asleep he could carry in groceries and baby stuff he'd bought in Grove.

For a second she fussed and he wondered if she'd wake up. But he remembered something he'd seen women at church do. He rocked the little seat, slow and easy. Lucy cuddled down into the blanket he'd gotten her and sucked on the pacifier.

"Yeah, that's right, I'm a pro at this. Now, don't wake up." He eased toward the door, avoiding spots on the hardwood floors that he knew were prone to creak.

When he got to the truck he could hear work going on at the construction site across the road. It looked as though some houses were going up on the fifty acres. He shrugged because it wasn't his land, just land he'd thought he might be able to buy.

He grabbed the baby bed out of the back of his truck and headed for the house, nearly tripping over a half-starved cat in the process. "Get out of here."

The cat yowled and ran for the barn. Feral cats. There were probably a dozen of them in the barn. He'd have to start catching them and taking them to the veterinarian in Dawson. One thing at a time. But he wasn't going to let a dozen cats keep reproducing in the one good thing about this property. The barn. He planned on turning that barn into his stable. And then he'd build a hay barn and equipment shed. He had plans. Dreams. His own this time.

As he carried the crib through the house he could hear the continued pounding from the other side of the road. The sound drifted through the open windows along with a nice breeze that felt a little cool for May. He set the crib in the larger of the two bedrooms, leaning it against the bed he'd bought used.

On his way back out to grab the remaining groceries, a cat ran in. He glanced back at the skinny gray tabby. He hated cats. He opened his mouth to yell at the scrawny feline and his attention landed on the sleeping baby in the seat.

Okay, his life as he knew it had ended. In one fell swoop, Becka had delivered the ultimate blow. She'd officially sidelined him, stolen his man-card and parked him square in the role of fatherhood. He didn't even get to yell at the cat that had meandered into the dining room and was sniffing the corner of the bare room.

"Later, cat." He whispered the threat and backed out the door, giving the cat the look and then pointing two fingers at his own eyes and then back at it, as if it would understand.

Ten minutes later he had groceries and baby paraphernalia in the house and even had the supplies stored in the three cabinets he'd cleaned out with window cleaner and paper towels. He looked around, not really pleased but okay with the cleaning job.

This little kitchen held a lot of memories, most had to do with his grandmother. He'd eaten a lot of fried bologna sandwiches and homemade chocolate chip cookies in this kitchen. Back then the cabinets had been painted bright yellow and the floor had been white-and-yellow linoleum. He didn't know if he'd return to that color scheme but he was looking forward to cleaning things up and making it look the way it used to.

A car driving fast down the country road caught his attention. He hurried to the door just in time to hear a dozen pops, similar to a small-caliber handgun. People across the road yelled. Someone shouted, "No housing project!"

Keeton started out the door, made it halfway to his truck and remembered the baby. He hurried back to the house, banging the front door as he rushed into the room and grabbed the infant carrier. The cat got smart and hightailed it out through a hole in the screen. The mangy thing didn't have a tail.

The strap in the truck played stubborn and it took him a few minutes to get the car seat belted into the truck. After that it only took minutes to get to the building site across the road. A couple of trucks were parked close and a woman stood near the corner of the new foundation making a phone call. She was tall, slim, dressed in a business suit and heels.

No way.

But yes way. She turned around and he was staring at the very lovely Sophie Cooper. She turned her back to him and walked away, still talking on the phone.

Next to him, Lucy cried out, demanding his attention. He leaned over and unbuckled her. When he pulled her out, she settled into the curve of his shoulder as if she'd always been there, made for that spot. It kind of hit him in the heart, how right it felt to hold a baby he'd only known for a few days.

He walked across the grassy field toward the foundation of a house.

"What happened?" he asked one of the men walking around the area, looking for whatever had been thrown at them. Or aimed at them.

The older of the two looked to be a few years younger than Keeton. Shaggy beard and a sweat-stained ball cap, the guy shrugged. "Guess they don't want us here."

"Did you see if they shot at you or threw something?"

The guy shrugged. "I think they threw fireworks. Ms. Cooper thought it was a gun."

Keeton smiled and so did the younger man. They walked around the area, looking for remnants of fireworks. He found them closer to the road than the house site. He left them for the police, assuming that's who Sophie had been on the phone with.

He walked back up to the house. There were

two trucks, no sedan. Sophie stood near one of the trucks, a beater in worse shape than his. So, she'd been going incognito. He smiled and then laughed.

"You're a contractor now?"

She bristled and took a step back. Man, she was beautiful. The wind whipped her hair around her face and she pushed it back with a gloved hand. Yeah, he liked Sophie the contractor. Even if she didn't want anything to do with Keeton the bull rider.

"I'm helping people build houses. I didn't exactly want it known." She pushed a hand through her hair and looked away. "And I am on the board of Cooper Holdings. I know how to get things done."

"Sophie, you're in Dawson, Oklahoma. Or at least close enough. People are going to find out. Did you really think you could keep something like this a secret?"

She shrugged slim shoulders beneath a clean, blue jacket. She must have gone home and changed after their encounter a few hours ago.

"I don't know. I guess I had hoped to keep it to myself. I keep my truck in the garage. No one knows I have it."

"You're a very sneaky woman." But he wondered aloud, "Why all the secrecy? It isn't as if you're doing something wrong. Are you?"

She glanced around the property, green with spring rains and warm sunshine. Wildflowers bloomed and the trees were heavy with new leaves. "No, I'm not doing anything wrong. I'm doing something for myself, without everyone in the world being involved."

"Gotcha." But he didn't really get it. He guessed if she wanted to explain, she would.

"The police are going to be here in a little while."

"Yeah, we found the remnants of fireworks."

Pink shaded her cheeks. "Well, it sounded like a gun."

"Why do they want to stop you from building?"

"I guess they don't like the idea of a subdivision."

He glanced around at the gravel drive leading into the place, the tall grass and the ropes used to plot out lots.

"Why do you have a subdivision listed as a nonprofit?"

"It is nonprofit." She sighed and took the squirming, fussy baby from his shoulder. "She's still warm."

"I know. I bought her fever reducer. As soon as I get to the house I'll give her some."

"Right." Sophie whispered to the baby that it would be all better. He kind of wished she'd whisper that to him. Instead she looked up, and when she met his gaze, her smile was gone and her eyes lacked something important. "Keeton, this started as a way for me to help some of our employees. There are good people trying to buy homes, buy places in the country to raise their kids, and they can't afford to. I bought the land, pooled people with different talents who want to build their own home and brought them all together to help each other build houses at cost. The Amish do it, why can't we?"

"And you're financing this?" Which might explain why she didn't want her family to know.

"No, not completely. I found a resource for low-interest loans."

"You're pretty amazing." He watched her with the baby, watched the way she cuddled the child as if it was the easiest thing in the world.

And he couldn't even get Lucy to take a nap without driving her around in his truck.

Now what? He needed to head back to his house, out of this mess. But he couldn't walk away. Why? He shrugged it off. Either he was staying because of her. Or because he owed it to Kade to look out for her.

If Kade had lived, Sophie would have been his sister-in-law. So yeah, he was doing it for his brother.

* * *

A police car came down the road, giving Sophie a break from the conversation with Keeton. She untangled herself from the smelly little bundle that was Lucy and handed the infant back to her daddy.

"You have to give her a bath today." She released the baby to her father's arms.

"Yeah, I know."

"You can do this, Keeton."

"I know." He cradled the now wide-awake baby in one arm. Sophie tried not to think about how he looked with that baby. "They really do have how-to books. I bought one at the store."

She shook her head at his admission. "That will help a lot."

"I'm sure it will." He walked next to her as the patrol car pulled in. "Want me to stay?"

"You can go."

He shifted the baby from his left arm to his right. "Suit yourself."

"I'm a big girl."

"I know you are. Just saying, I'm here if you need anything."

"I know you are. And—" she smiled at the baby then raised her gaze to meet his "—I'm just down the road if you need anything."

The words weren't easy. She almost hadn't

said them. But it was the right thing to do, offering help.

"Thanks." He touched the brim of his hat. "See you at the rodeo tonight?"

"Probably not."

She watched as he got into his truck and started down the bumpy, gravel drive. Today, nothing made sense. Keeton back in town didn't make sense. Her reaction to seeing him made less sense. Even when she made the point to remind herself he was just another cowboy in faded jeans and dusty boots her heart waffled, not really agreeing.

Maybe because he hadn't teased her. He hadn't questioned what she was doing and why. She watched him go, biting her bottom lip until it hurt. And then the officer approached, casting a cautious gaze around the area.

"Ms. Cooper?"

"Yes." She turned, giving him her full attention. For the most part.

"I'm Officer Walters."

They leaned against her truck as she recounted the story, ending with an apology for calling him out on something as silly as firecrackers.

"Ma'am, if you felt threatened by their actions, then that's exactly why you should have called. We'll have something on record in case there are other incidents, and if we see a pattern."

"That sounds good." Though she couldn't imagine what pattern they'd see. Fireworks didn't match a criminal profile that she knew of. It appeared to be more a case of overactive imagination on her part.

Jeff and Gabe told what they remembered, and then they took the police officer to the spot where they'd found the firecrackers. She watched as he shoved the evidence into a plastic bag and walked back up to where she waited.

"I've got a description of the car and what you think the passenger looked like. I'll take this in and we'll call you if we find anything. If you do see that car again, call. And if you can get a license number without putting yourself in danger, that would help."

"Thank you, Officer." Sophie watched him leave, and then she glanced at her watch. It was almost two o'clock on a Saturday afternoon. The two guys standing in front of her looked as if they would rather be anywhere but here.

"What now, Ms. Cooper?" Jeff, tall and lanky, picked up his tool bag and strapped it around his waist. He pushed his ball cap down on thinning hair.

"Let's go home, guys. The supplies are here. If the two of you and a few others want to do more on the frame next week, everything is ready to go."

"That sounds good." Gabe picked up the toolbox he'd left near her truck. "Call if you need anything at all."

"Thanks, Gabe." She smiled at the younger man. He was single and unemployed for the time being so he had signed on to help a few of his married friends build houses. His experience in so many areas of construction made him a valuable part of the team.

After the two of them left she got into the old truck she'd bought a few weeks ago. She eased down the gravel drive, and at the road she didn't turn toward her house. Instead she turned left, and then into the driveway of the old West homestead.

Keeton's truck was parked close to the front door. She sat for a minute staring at the old farmhouse with the dark green siding. She'd loved this place years ago when his grandparents were alive. It always reminded her of trees in the summer. Dark green with brown trim around the windows and brown shingles. Irises bloomed profusely around the house, leftovers from tubers his grandmother had planted. When she bought her house a few years ago, she'd dug up several and replanted them around her front porch.

The front door opened. Keeton walked out and then leaned against the post. She laughed because he looked cool, pretty cute, actually. Until the post he chose to lean against wobbled and came loose. He fell to the side and righted himself.

His smile zoomed across the yard, bright with white teeth that flashed.

"You getting out?" he called out to her.

She shouldn't. Not if she had any sense at all. She'd always been the Cooper kid most likely to use common sense. Lately something had happened. Maybe an early midlife crisis?

Instead of waving goodbye and leaving, she got out. Her heart raced ahead of her. And then guilt rushed in. It ached deep down, tangling with the past and with this moment.

"Don't look like you just stole the teacher's apple."

"Why would a teacher ever really want an apple?" Was that the only thing she could come back with? "I mean, really, wouldn't she be glad if someone took it? Wouldn't she prefer a student give her chocolate?"

"You're overthinking this."

She cleared her throat and nodded. "Of course I am. I'm Sophie Cooper, I always overthink."

"Right, and where has that gotten you?"

For a moment she thought about that question. But then she heard the baby from inside the house, crying. "I think someone wants you."

"Right. Are you coming in?" He headed toward the house, not waiting for her. "You didn't answer. Where has overthinking gotten you?"

He glanced back over his shoulder as he walked up the steps of the porch.

"Overthinking has kept me out of trouble." And kept her heart virtually pain free for sixteen years. Poor atrophied heart. It needed serious physical therapy if she ever planned on using it again.

She followed Keeton through the front door. He had already picked up Lucy and had her cradled against his chest. "She's pretty warm."

Sophie kissed the baby's brow. "Very. Have you given her the medicine?"

"Yeah, when I got back."

"And a bath?"

"Not yet." He smiled and there was something different about a cowboy smile when the cowboy was holding a baby. "I haven't read the book."

Sophie reached for the baby and he handed Lucy over.

"Run lukewarm water in the sink. We'll start there. I'll give you a crash course in baby bathing and you can read your how-to manual later."

"Thanks, Sophie, I owe you."

"No, you don't." She followed him into the kitchen. He turned on the tap and washed out the sink. "Do you have baby soap?"

"Yeah, let me get the water going and I'll go get the supplies I bought at the store."

Regret—Sophie had a lot. And after today, she'd have more. Hip against the counter, she watched as he plugged the sink and then rummaged through the plastic bags on the counter, pulling out the soap, washcloth and towel. He held up a little sleeper, pink with ponies on the front.

"Sweet. You did good." Sophie spread the towel on the counter and slipped off the dirty sleeper. She dropped it on the floor and waited for it to get up and walk away on its own. It was that dirty.

"Now what?"

"You can throw that sleeper away."

"Done." He picked it up and tossed it in the trash. A second later he was at her side again. He smelled good. Spicy with a hint of a pine forest mixed in. It was the kind of scent that made a woman want to lean in close.

If it were any other man. If she was any other woman. She sighed and let go of need, held on to strength.

"In the bath she goes." Sophie lifted the baby, and before putting her in the water, tested it to make sure it wasn't too hot or cold. "Perfect. Maybe this will help break that fever. And I'm sure she'll feel better."

"Soph, I appreciate this."

"Of course you do, because you think I'm going to do all of the work. Surprise." She cradled the baby in the water. Lucy tested the surface of the water with pudgy little fingers, and then she splashed just a little. "Hold her like this and then squirt a little soap on the washcloth. It doesn't take much to wash a baby, Keeton. Even her hair. There isn't much of it."

"Right, of course." He swallowed loud and she looked up, smiling at the bead of perspiration across his brow.

"Easy-peasy." She moved a little but still cradled the baby on her left arm. "Your turn."

"She's already clean."

"I know, but I want you to be able to do this on your own."

"I can." He cleared his throat. "Seriously, Soph, I can do this."

"You could hire a nanny."

"I have skills."

Yeah, she thought.

He reached for his baby girl and Sophie moved her hands to make room for his. She glanced up and he looked down. It felt suddenly very warm in that little kitchen.

"I can handle it without a nanny." He repeated her actions and Lucy giggled, happy to be clean and to be cooler. "She hasn't eaten a lot today."

"She needs liquids. Especially now, with a fever. If she gets enough formula, give her water." She placed the towel over his shoulder and he looked a little stricken. "Take her out before she gets chilled."

"I can't believe this is my life." He lifted Lucy out of the bathwater and wrapped the towel around her. Sophie took the child from his arms.

"Believe it, Keeton West, this is your life." She held Lucy close. "What were you planning, coming back here?"

He grabbed a diaper and the sleeper. Sophie put the baby on the counter and made quick work of putting a diaper and the sleeper on Lucy. A little part of her liked that he looked in awe.

"I thought I'd come back and reclaim what should have been mine." He held his daughter.

The lighthearted moment of seconds ago dissolved. "I'm sorry."

"It wasn't your fault." He leaned, brushing a brotherly kiss on the side of her head. She paused midbutton on the sleeper and looked up at him.

"I know it isn't—wasn't my fault. I'm sorry, Keeton, for everything. I'm sorry for the years we've all lost, being sorry, being guilty, being alone." She looked away, because it was easier to focus on Lucy. "It wasn't your fault."

"I know."

Did he really? She thought he probably still

felt guilty. He'd been a kid, really. Even though at eighteen and nineteen they'd thought they were grown, thought they knew everything.

She handed him the baby girl that had his eyes. And in those eyes she saw a little bit of Kade, the West she'd planned on marrying. In a jewelry box at home she had the ring he'd given her, a promise that someday they'd get engaged, get married.

She also had a rose, taken from one of the flower arrangements on his casket. And in a notebook, hidden away in her dresser, she had a note from Keeton, telling her how sorry he was for what had happened. He blamed himself. He would always blame himself.

And he'd spent his life trying to earn the national bull-riding championship Kade had wanted. He was still chasing Kade's dreams.

She wanted to tell him that. She wanted to tell him to let it go and find what he wanted. Maybe this farm was it? But she wouldn't go back to other memories, of the afternoon of the funeral and finding comfort in Keeton's arms.

Keeton wasn't the only one who felt guilty.

Chapter Three

Keeton walked Sophie out the front door. Lucy, bathed and cooler to the touch, slept soundly in her new crib. Sophie had promised to watch his daughter while he rode at a local bull ride that evening. He'd brought it up. She'd offered. For the baby, not for him.

A crash in the field caught his attention as they stood on the porch. He glanced toward the barn, saw a flash of red-gold.

"What's that?"

Sophie looked in the direction he pointed and she laughed. Okay, so whatever it was, she found it amusing. He watched as the animal tramped through the overgrown brush and scrub trees that he'd be cutting down in a few days. A mule appeared. It saw them, snorted, tossed its big head and then raced off in the other direction. Before Keeton could comment, the mule jumped the fallen tree that leaned against the corral.

"That was Lucky the mule." She shaded her eyes with her hand and watched. And he watched her.

"You find Lucky on the loose amusing?"

She turned, still smiling. The girl his brother had planned to marry still lurked in her eyes, still smiled up at him. But she was a woman. A beautiful woman. One he would have liked knowing. Would still like to know. That brought up a whole bag of "if only" that he didn't plan on getting into.

"Lucky belongs to my brother Lucky, but then, Lucky doesn't belong to anyone. Lucky, my brother, bought him six months ago, as a yearling. He brought him home, put him in the corral. The next day, Lucky was gone. Got that?"

"I think. Lucky your brother has a mule named Lucky, which you named. He's been running loose for six months?"

"Yep."

"Unbelievable." He turned his attention back to the field, looking for the mule. "Why don't they catch him?"

"They can't touch him."

"Gotcha." He followed her down the steps. "You sure you don't mind watching Lucy for me?"

"No, I don't mind. But I'm not going to watch you ride a bull."

"I won't get hurt."

She drew in a breath and turned away from him. Too late. He reached for her arm and she shook her head. "I'm going home, Keeton. I'll watch the baby."

"Soph, I'm sorry." He reached for her hand and drew her back to him. "I'm sorry."

"Keeton, let's stop this. We're both adults now. It was a long time ago. It hurt. But it hadn't hurt..."

"Until I came back."

"Yeah, something like that. Stop bringing it up. Stop apologizing. Stop living in the past. God doesn't want us living in the past. This is today. We have a life today that we need to concentrate on."

He wondered if she'd really been concentrating on living this life. He held her left hand, the one that had never worn a ring. For someone moving on, living in the present, she was doing a lot of holding on to the past.

But he was the last person who would lecture her on that. He was still riding bulls. He didn't love the sport. He didn't really care about the championship or world titles. For years he'd been trying to win the title his brother had wanted.

He'd been trying to put his family back together.

"Okay, no more apologizing." He smiled like

he meant it and she responded, like she meant it. And neither of them did.

Sophie sighed. "I have to go. Please don't tell my family about the land."

"Okay." He wanted to ask why, but he figured he got it. When a person grew up a Cooper, they didn't have much that was just theirs. Including secrets.

A few minutes later her truck pulled onto the road. Keeton walked back into the house. He stood in the living room, waiting for the past to stop rushing at him. As a little kid he'd spent a lot of time in this house until his grandparents had moved to town. He and Kade had spent summer nights on the front porch, hoping for a little breeze because there hadn't been air-conditioning in the house.

His grandma used to sit in a flowery chair in front of the window and fan herself with a magazine. He smiled, remembering images that hadn't been this clear in years. This house. This land. It had been a part of him. This house and the one down the road where he'd grown up. That house now belonged to a family named Matthews.

He'd driven past today and saw that there were bikes in the front yard, a basketball hoop and horses in the corral.

At twenty he'd helped his parents pack it all up and move to Tulsa. They hadn't been able to move on after losing Kade. They'd tried to get back to what had been their lives, and it hadn't happened. There'd been too much guilt, too many accusations and way too much pain.

He shook his head as he walked through the empty rooms. Paneled walls. Hardwood floors that sagged in places. It was livable but it needed a lot of work. And that mangy cat had slipped back inside. The thing yowled at him, wanting food. He opened a can of tuna and sat it on the floor.

"Don't get too comfortable in here, Mangy."

The cat yowled again. And then the baby cried. Keeton tossed his hat on the counter and walked down the hall to the bedroom. Lucy stopped crying when she saw him. He smiled at that.

He'd had her for two days. He'd known about her for two days. When he thought about how unfair that was, it made him madder than anything. Becka had kept him from the best thing in his life. He didn't really know what to do with a baby. But she definitely took the title for best thing ever.

The big question at the moment was how to be a bull rider and a single dad. That even put getting his land back from Sophie on hold, or made it less important somehow. He picked up his baby girl and held her close. She smelled a lot better.

"You smell good, little girl. I was afraid that other smell was permanent."

She smiled a soft baby smile and he held her easy in one arm while he reached for the bottle and the soft blanket. She felt warm again. He'd bought a book on babies and had read warnings about high fevers, but also about not rushing to the doctor for every virus. So how did he know what to do with that advice?

"What in the world are we going to do about this fever?"

She cooed and he knew at that moment that no one had better ever hurt his little girl. They'd have to deal with him.

He was a dad. A single dad in a house without furniture. A single dad without a significant other to give him a helping hand. He'd faced some pretty mean bulls over the years, but he'd never faced anything that frightened him as much as the prospect of raising one tiny little girl.

The thought spun around in his mind. He was now responsible for another person's future. A little person, yeah, but she wouldn't always be little.

Someday she'd be a teenager. She'd have boyfriends. He'd have to hurt them.

"Baby, you are never, ever going to date."

She cooed again and smiled a little. Yeah, in fifteen years she wouldn't be smiling at him like that. With that thought in his mind he started packing the diaper bag to take Lucy to Sophie.

Sophie crumpled the note she'd found on her door when she got back from Keeton's. But on second thought she smoothed it out and dropped it on the kitchen counter. Because, what if something happened?

A note warning her that she shouldn't build a subdivision on farmland might be of interest to the police. If something should happen. If. But it probably meant nothing. She couldn't think of a reason why her subdivision would upset anyone.

The only person slightly bothered by it would be Keeton, and only because the land had once belonged to his family.

Sophie opened a cabinet door and reached for her staple—peanut butter. She spread it on a slice of bread, then covered that with a layer of black-berry jam.

The perfect food.

She carried the one slice of bread with top-pings to the kitchen table and sat down, putting her feet up on the chair next to the one she sat on. Her home. Her life. No one to tell her to sit up straight, pull her hair back, eat healthy.

If she wanted to, she could listen to loud music all night. She could leave every light in the house on. She could wear her pajamas all day. Bonus, her sister Heather wasn't lurking, waiting to straighten pillows or make the bed. Although she did stop in from time to time with a new picture for the wall.

Being an adult meant no more sharing. No more brothers and sisters poking around in her life. No man cluttering things up.

No more quiet secrets at night after everyone went to bed. Yes, she did miss that part. She missed that Heather had always been there for her. She missed Mia's silly stories.

But she loved peace and quiet. Her own space.

The picture on the table next to her mocked her with its silliness. Her new sister-in-law Madeline had given her the photograph in a silver frame, a thank-you for helping with Madeline and Jackson's wedding. A picture of Sophie fumbling as the bouquet Madeline tossed practically fell into her arms. She pushed the picture facedown and snarled at it.

As she finished off the last bite of sandwich she heard tires crunching on gravel and the low hum of an engine. She leaned to peek out the front screen door, saw that it was Keeton and relaxed. But then she panicked. She looked down at the sweatpants she'd cut off at the knees and the crazy tie-dyed T-shirt she'd changed into when she got home.

She jumped and ran down the hall, a surge of

panic shooting adrenaline through her veins. She would not get caught like this.

Before she could put her plate in the sink and make it through the living room to the stairs that led to her bedroom, Keeton stood at the front door. He grinned through the screen door and wiggled two fingers. In his other arm he held the precious bundle that was his daughter.

Two reactions. She wanted to run and hide. She wanted to stop and stare at the man on her front porch. She had to act quickly.

"Come in, I'm going to change."

He stepped in before she could run. "Why?"

But he smirked a cute little grin and gave her the once-over. She should point out that he needed to shave and his worn-out jeans were in need of replacing. She walked away from him, knowing he'd follow.

"What's going on?"

Coffee. She needed a cup of coffee. She walked down the hall to the kitchen. Keeton's boots clunked on the wood floor. If she gave herself a few minutes she could face him and not be at loose ends. She didn't do this, this chaotic dance around men—insecure, uncertain. Sophie Cooper knew how to be confident.

She reached for the coffeepot, saw the note on the counter. Before he could reach her she grabbed it and slipped it in her pocket.

"Do you want coffee?"

Keeton held Lucy out to her. "Yeah, I want coffee. I'll make it because I also don't want to pick up glass from the broken coffeepot when you drop it. What's up with you?"

Keeton. A crazy note on her front door. She didn't know where to start. She didn't want to start.

Rather than answering, she took Lucy and sat down at the butcher-block table in the center of the kitchen. Lucy, soft and smelling of lavender and chamomile, cooed. She still felt warm.

"I'm worried about this baby."

Keeton looked back at them, and then poured water into the coffeepot. "I gave her the medicine. I don't know what else to do."

"Maybe urgent care."

"Yeah, I think I might need to do that. Let's stop beating around the bush. Why don't you tell me about that piece of paper you slipped in your pocket when you thought I wasn't looking?"

"Paper?" Heat warmed her neck and then her cheeks.

"You're a horrible liar."

"I know." She leaned her forehead against Lucy's. "Sweet baby, you need to get over this virus."

"Note."

"Baby trumps note. We need to take her to the doctor."

"We?" He leaned against the counter, his elbows behind him resting on the counter top. He wasn't particularly tall. Most bull riders weren't. He appeared tall. Maybe that unbelievable self-confidence the West men oozed. She sighed. Kade had had it, too.

She wondered what kind of man he'd have been if he'd lived. Would they have gotten married? Or would they have grown up in a few years and realized it was just a crush?

"Soph? About the note? And then we'll talk about Lucy and the doctor."

"The note warned me to stop building a subdivision on farmland."

"I didn't write it."

"I know you didn't." She looked up, making strong eye contact with him. "I know you didn't."

"Good. But we have to find out who did. I want to know that you're safe here."

"I'm safe. I'm a Cooper. I can fight with the best of them. And shoot a gun."

He grinned and shook his head. Without asking, he pulled cups out of the cabinet and started pouring coffee. "Sugar?"

"Nope."

"Black coffee." He glanced back again. "And you have peanut butter on your chin."

She rubbed fast, and then wiped her fingers on a napkin. "I don't."

"You have so many surprising little habits, Sophie." He carried two cups of coffee and sat down across from her. "I figured if it's a virus she'll run a fever for a couple of days and be over it. Right? Antibiotics won't cure a virus."

"I suppose. But she's so little, I worry about her fever getting too high."

"I've been keeping an eye on that. So far it's stayed under 102."

"I'd make her an appointment tomorrow, then. If she isn't better."

"Thanks, Soph. So will you still watch her for me tonight while I go ride bulls in Dawson?"

That's why he was there. She'd somehow managed to forget. She snuggled the baby and thought about rocking her to sleep, the two of them dozing on the sofa together. Keeton's baby, not hers. She felt a little alone for a moment, even with the two of them right there with her. Because they weren't hers.

"I'll watch her."

"I have a can of formula and extra diapers in the diaper bag."

"Okay." She stood when he stood. "Be careful tonight."

He plucked at a strand of her hair and nodded

once. "I will. I always am. Soph, it hardly ever happens that way—the way it did…"

"I know." And she didn't usually cry. But her eyes burned and if he didn't leave, she would.

He didn't leave. Instead he leaned and sweetly kissed her. She closed her eyes and for a moment she needed this, needed him. She resurfaced when memories of another moment in his arms pushed their way into her mind.

Before she could make sense of it all, he stepped back. One simple kiss and he undid all of her carefully groomed self-control. She couldn't allow that.

She gathered herself, her wits, and stood a little straighter.

"Keeton, don't."

He tipped his hat. "I know."

"We can't."

"I know." His smile didn't beam this time, instead it looked a little sad, a little sorry. And so was she. "I know."

He walked down the hall back to the front door. She followed him. "Keeton, it isn't you."

At the front door he turned, smiling again. "It's never been me."

"That isn't what I meant." But it was. And wasn't. She was making a royal mess of things. The baby whimpered against her shoulder and

Keeton walked out the door, letting it thud behind him.

"Goodbye," she whispered, and then she whispered a prayer. "God, keep him safe."

What if he got hurt? Then what? What about the baby? She rushed out the door, wanting to stop him, to tell him he had a little girl and something could happen to him. Too late, his truck pulled out onto the road and turned in the direction of Dawson.

"It's you and me, baby girl. And we're going to be doing lots of praying tonight."

Chapter Four

The Dawson Rodeo Grounds hadn't changed much over the years. Keeton liked that about Dawson, that it didn't change. It hadn't gotten sucked up in urban sprawl. Mainly because there wasn't an urban area close enough. Sometimes they got lost tourists looking for Grand Lake. Mostly, it was just Dawson and the folks who'd been here for generations. He liked the slow pace of life, knowing neighbors, knowing the roads, the houses and what made people tick.

Not that he could figure out Sophie Cooper. Each time he thought he had her pegged, she shifted and left him scratching his head.

He pulled into the grassy parking area of the arena and parked next to a beater that had seen better days. His old truck was in similar shape but he had a new one on the way. As he stepped out of his pickup a voice shouted his name. He turned and waved at Jeremy Hightree. It was thanks to Jeremy and his skill with bikes that Keeton had money saved up to buy back his family spread.

The money would stay in the bank for now, because he'd only been able to purchase the twenty that his grandparents' home sat on.

Jeremy headed his way. "I guess you really are back?"

"I'm back." He reached into his truck for chaps and a bull rope.

"So, rumor has it you've got a kid." Jeremy leaned against the side of Keeton's truck, pretending to fiddle with the strap on his chaps. Keeton figured Jeremy was more than a little interested because of his own past. He was Sophie's half brother. A Cooper, and he hadn't known that fact for most of his life.

"I guess I do."

"Kind of a surprise, wasn't it?"

Keeton looked up. "Jeremy, *surprise* doesn't even begin to explain it."

"Where is she?"

Now, how did he get out of answering that question? Might as well answer because odds were, Jeremy and most of Dawson knew where Lucy was. "Sophie's watching her."

Jeremy grinned big, the way Keeton had kind

of guessed he would. "That's good. She's probably a great babysitter."

"Right." Keeton coiled his bull rope and walked away. "Later."

Of course Jeremy followed him. "Do you need any help over at the old homestead?"

Now, that question had merit. "Probably in the next few days. I'm going to have to patch the roof, replace a couple of windows and probably rebuild the porch."

At that, Jeremy laughed. "I meant do you want me to bring you a casserole or something. I hadn't really planned on hard labor."

"You can bring me a casserole and help me patch the roof."

"I suppose I could." Jeremy pointed to a man in black jeans and a white shirt. "Dave has the list, he'll let you know when you're up and what bull you're on."

"Thanks."

And then Jeremy laughed, his attention focused on the parking lot. "Well, what do you know? Is that Sophie parking her car?"

"Never."

"No, I'm sure it is." Jeremy pointed to the big sedan and the woman getting out.

Gone were her pretty amazing sweatpants and the tie-dyed T-shirt. Back was the Sophie in business formal. She had his baby in her arms.

It shouldn't feel so perfect, seeing her with his baby. But everything about this was out of place. Sophie in her dress slacks and blouse. Lucy in her arms. His life had somehow gotten shaken up to the point that he didn't recognize it as his life.

"See you later." Jeremy slapped his back and walked away.

"Right." Keeton walked toward Sophie. She smiled a little and held Lucy close. "What are you doing here? Is Lucy okay?"

"Lucy still has a little fever." She bit down on her bottom lip, and then looked up, letting him see tears in her hazel eyes. He had a hard time not pulling her close. He stood his ground, though, waiting for her explanation.

"What's wrong?"

She sniffled. He'd never seen her as the type to get emotional over nothing. She raised her chin a notch and got control back.

"I couldn't sit there and wait for you to come home. I kept thinking about you being here, riding bulls. And Lucy. She's so little. What if…"

Even with the glimmer of tears, her voice remained strong.

He stopped her with a slight shake of his head. "Don't. Nothing is going to happen to me."

"This doesn't count toward the finals. You don't have to ride here."

"I want to ride here."

He used to want to ride here. He wanted to be seventeen again, living his dream, waking up each morning to a family that was whole. For some crazy reason he kept thinking he could get that back. His parents, his brother, his life.

Buying the land had been the plan. The way to get his life back.

Sophie stared at him, as if she knew exactly what thoughts were going through his mind. And she looked sorry, for her and for him.

"Sophie, this is what I do. I ride bulls."

"I know."

He wanted to hold her but he knew she wouldn't want that. She had her stronger-than-steel look on her face. She wouldn't melt. She wouldn't fall apart.

"So wish me luck?"

"Of course, luck. And some prayers." She swayed with Lucy in her arms. "I thought it would be easier to watch instead of being at home worrying, not knowing."

"I understand." He let out a sigh as they announced bull riding directly after barrel racing. "I've got to go."

"I'll find a place to sit."

"Soph—" he stepped close because he couldn't just walk away "—she looks good in your arms."

Before she could protest or call him a choice name, he walked away. But he couldn't stop smiling. Not even when they told him which bull he'd be riding. He'd drawn one of the meanest bulls the Coopers owned.

Jackson Cooper grinned, and then laughed. "You sure you don't want to take a sick day, Keet?"

"I can ride this bull with my eyes closed."

"I think you'll want your eyes closed and some serious prayers before you ride him." Jackson walked away from the fence he'd been leaning against. His smile disappeared. Great.

"I can handle him, Jackson."

"I know you can. But tell me this. What are you doing with Sophie?"

"She's watching Lucy for me. That's all."

"Mind a little advice?"

Keeton shrugged and pretended this conversation meant nothing. But Jackson had a pretty serious look on his face that warned him to tread easy. "Sure."

"Don't hurt her."

"I'm not planning on it. She's always been a friend."

"I think we both know that isn't true."

"Jackson, there's been a lot of years lived since Kade passed. There's been a lot of time and distance."

"I know. And here you both are, still stuck in the past."

"I'm not stuck in the past."

"You're here because you can't let go."

"I'm here to get back what I lost."

Jackson's eyes narrowed dangerously. "Sophie's on the list of things you lost?"

"No, Sophie was never on the list of things I had to lose."

At thirty-six, he was too stinking old for this conversation. He pushed his hat back and looked Jackson Cooper straight in the eye. "Jackson, with all due respect, back off."

"She's my sister."

"We're not teenagers. She's not a kid you have to watch over. I don't have to declare my intentions like this is some Old West drama."

Jackson laughed. "You have intentions?"

"I have to ride a bull. And then I plan on ignoring you."

He walked past Jackson and climbed the steps to the platform where he would wait to get on his bull. The old Holstein bull the Coopers owned bellowed in his chute, raising off his front legs in an attempt to climb out of the metal enclosure.

It kind of made a guy wonder why he did this

for a living. It also kept him praying. But his attention strayed to the stands, looking for Sophie with his little girl. He spotted them. Sophie sat near the bottom of the bleachers, next to a woman he didn't know. She had a cola in one hand and his baby in her arms.

Things had definitely changed. For the better? Yeah, he thought so.

Sophie hadn't attended a rodeo in years. She never watched bull riding. Tonight she had to. She'd tried cuddling up with Lucy, pretending she didn't care. But after thirty minutes at home, thinking about Keeton on a bull, she couldn't take it. She had to be here, to watch. As if being here would stop something bad from happening.

She knew whatever would happen would happen with or without her presence. She knew that God really could take care of things without her help.

But logic had obviously flown out the window, along with common sense and a few other personal strengths. At this point, emotion seemed to be in control. And when had that ever happened to her?

Okay, not a question she wanted to answer.

She resituated herself on the wooden bench and pretended she really didn't care what happened in the arena. She didn't care that Dylan, her little brother, had just settled onto the back of a bull.

Travis, older than Dylan by a couple of years, stood in the arena, ready to rescue their little brother if need be. Jackson had the role of pick-up guy, sitting on his big chestnut gelding, reins loose in his hands, but the horse in control.

Sophie's new sister-in-law Elizabeth leaned close. "It really will be okay."

Sophie nodded but she couldn't ask Elizabeth what she knew. Elizabeth was sweet. She was kind; she wanted to comfort Sophie. And she knew very little of the turmoil inside Sophie at that moment.

"I know."

Elizabeth reached for her hand. "I'll pray, too."

Sophie nodded again and this time she couldn't answer. The gate flew open. Sophie had always thought of herself as a strong person. She knew how to work past her pain, how to get things done.

She closed her eyes as her little brother came spinning out of the chute on the back of a bull. She squeezed them tighter when she heard the crowd scream. Elizabeth's hand on hers held tight.

Two seconds into the ride, she opened her eyes and watched as Dylan slid to the side of the mammoth bull and then righted himself with his free arm, getting himself back in place. Her heart thudded hard and she held her breath. The buzzer sounded.

Dylan flew through the air, landing hard on his back. He shook his head, and then jumped, running from the bull that had decided playtime wasn't over. Travis distracted the animal, tossing his hat to get its attention and giving Dylan a precious few seconds to jump over the gate.

"That cowboy gets a score." The announcer spoke over the old PA system that crackled and cut a syllable or two from the announcement. "Dylan Cooper, 85.4."

Sophie would have clapped but she had Lucy in her arms and the baby had fallen asleep. Next to her, Elizabeth clapped quietly, smiling at the sleeping infant.

The next rider up, Keeton West. The emcee gave a brief rundown of Keeton's standings in the bid for a world title. He talked about Keeton's past. He didn't mention Kade. She looked up at the announcer's box and smiled at Mike Farrows, a longtime resident of Dawson and often emcee of the rodeo. He tipped his hat and smiled back.

A commotion in the chute caught her attention. She watched as Keeton settled onto the back of his bull, one owned by her family. The old animal had seen better days, some said, but he could still put a guy on the ground. And make it hard for him to get settled and get his hand tight before the gate even opened.

"I can't watch." She stood up, ignoring the look Elizabeth gave her. "I have to go."

"I'll go with…" Elizabeth stood to follow her.

"Stay." Sophie smiled, letting Elizabeth off the hook. "I'm fine. I just can't watch."

But the chute opened and she didn't have a choice. Behind her, people wanted to see the action. She sat back down and waited, reminding herself that God could handle this. Of course He could. "Who, by worrying, can add a cubit to his stature," she reminded herself. What good did worry do? It didn't solve problems, cure illness, fix pain. Worry just added to troubles, made them bigger, more difficult.

She could… The buzzer sounded. Keeton jumped. He landed funny, going down on one knee. The bull charged. She held her breath, waiting. One of the bull fighters pulled Keeton back, and then Travis jumped in the way, somehow going airborne and flying over the back of the bull. The second bull fighter pulled the bull's horns and distracted the animal from going after Travis. Keeton had already made it safely through the gate.

And of course Travis didn't get hurt. He rarely did. Next to Sophie, Elizabeth exhaled and slumped a little. "He scares me when he does that."

"I know." Sophie reached for Elizabeth's hand but she watched Keeton limp from the arena. "I know."

She let go of Elizabeth's hand and excused herself. With Lucy held tight she picked her way through the crowd, and then headed for the back of the arena where cowboys stood talking in small groups, laughing, acting as if nothing had happened.

Keeton sat on the tailgate of a truck, his jean leg pulled up to expose a swollen knee. He grinned when she walked up, but something on her face must have warned him. His smile faded.

"Just a bruise," he explained with a little bit of his smile back.

"Right. Idiot."

"I guess I deserve that. For whatever reason."

"You're thirty-six and still riding bulls. Figure it out."

"Yeah, I guess it's about time to retire." He eased himself down from the truck. "But I think I won first place tonight. So maybe I'll wait another day or two."

"Good idea."

He winked and slid an arm around her waist. "I'm surprised you care so much."

"I care because you have a daughter and what if something happens to you?"

"So this isn't about you and me?"

"Stop joking around." Sophie pulled away from him, Lucy still in her arms. The baby slept through everything.

Keeton didn't smile. He didn't grin. He didn't wink. Instead he tilted his head to the side and stared at her, as if he had just seen her for the first time. "Soph, I'm not sure I'm teasing. Maybe I want this to be about you and me. What would you say to that?"

"I'd say you hit your head when you fell off that bull."

He did grin after that. "I didn't hit my head."

"You're losing your mind."

He stepped close to her side and leaned in a little. "I'm thinking very clearly."

"Keeton, stop."

"I'm not sure if I can. Sophie, you know I've always…"

She put a hand up to stop him. But instead of doing what she intended, he slipped his fingers through hers and pulled her hand down to his side, pulling her close. "Keeton."

"Give me a chance to be the man you need. I'm not a boy. We're not kids." He didn't smile now, and she knew this would be tough. "This has to be said, Sophie. Kade's gone. This isn't about him, it's about us."

"I loved him."

"I know you did. He was my kid brother and I loved him, too. But all of these years, loving someone who is gone."

"Making his dreams yours?" she added.

"Maybe. But us, that's something different. This is different."

"I can't." She couldn't think. She couldn't breathe. She couldn't let him have space in her heart. No vacancy.

"I'm not giving up."

She put Lucy in his arms. "I'm leaving. I can't do this."

"You can't run from it."

"Yes, I can." She could be a coward if it meant protecting her heart from a cowboy who wouldn't stay in her life. "See you around."

"You have the infant seat."

"Come and get it." She kept walking, her back to him.

"Soph, come on."

She turned back and he stood in the same spot, a cowboy in a dusty shirt, worn chaps, and his hat pushed back. The baby curled in his arms seemed out of place, and yet, not. "What."

"I think I can't walk that fast on this knee." He grinned. "And that isn't easy to admit."

"Fine." She walked back and took Lucy from his arms. "I'll carry her. You're on your own."

"Thanks." He limped next to her as they walked across the parking area to her car.

Sophie slowed to match his uneven gait. "Do you need to go to the emergency room?"

"No, I'm fine. It's an old wound that I keep hoping will fix itself. Torn ACL."

"Brilliant. Did you think of maybe having surgery?"

"Not this season. Not when I'm this high up in the standings."

"So you'll…" She shook her head and let it go. "Never mind. Do what you want."

"Thank you, I will." He leaned against her car as she held Lucy in one arm and pulled the seat out with the other. "I can take her."

Sophie handed him the seat. "I'll get her in the truck for you."

"This hurts a little more than it used to," he admitted as they walked to his truck.

"I'm sure it does. That's because you're old."

"Do you have to keep reminding me of that?"

"Someone should." She opened the truck door and he put the seat in. "But you're still pretty easy to look at."

And she really *had* just said that. She wanted to groan as the words slipped out, bringing his head up as he fastened the seat into the truck.

Of course he smiled an easy smile, his dark eyes locking with hers.

"You're pretty easy on the eyes, too." He took the baby from her arms. "As a matter of fact, you're pretty easy to hold."

"Don't make me sorry I said that." She already was.

He laughed as he buckled Lucy into her seat. "Soph, you're sorry without me helping."

The baby woke up, fussed a little and went back to sleep. Keeton closed the truck door and Sophie found herself still standing there. She should walk away. She should mean what she said about not wanting him in her life.

But she hadn't meant it and they both knew it.

"I'm going." She hadn't meant that, either.

Keeton touched her hand and then he held it, using the touch to draw her to him. One step and they were face-to-face. One motion and she was in his arms. One heartbeat, two. His lips on hers. Her arms around his waist. His arms holding her tight. Years melted. She remembered being seventeen and knowing that no one else would ever make her feel what Keeton West made her feel. She remembered the guilt in that moment.

He whispered her name close to her ear. Sophie opened her eyes, shaking her head in response and to clear her thoughts.

"I have to go."

"I wish you wouldn't."

"I have to go." She walked away and she didn't look back, because looking back was never a good idea. The cowboy Cupid seemed to be on the loose again. She would not get struck by his arrow.

Chapter Five

The alarm clock went off way too soon. Keeton groaned and rolled over to slap the snooze button. Lucy whimpered. He hit the button fast. She'd been awake twice in the night. He couldn't make it through the day if he didn't get a little sleep.

A few minutes later it went off again. He opened one eye and glanced at the time. Nearly eight in the morning. He had to get up and get busy. He'd figured on going to church today. That's what a guy did when he moved back home to Dawson. He moved into his old home, renewed old friendships, maybe found his old faith.

Renewed old friendships. That thought brought another and he covered his face with his arm. Sophie. He moved his arm and looked out the window, wondering what in the world he'd been thinking the night before. He shouldn't have kissed her. He definitely shouldn't have held her.

Holding her had been the biggest mistake. A kiss could almost be nothing. Holding Sophie, that changed everything. Holding her was personal. It connected them. Or at least connected him. She might take more convincing.

The phone rang. He reached for it, drawing it to his ear.

"Yeah."

"It's Mom."

"Oh. Hi."

"Why in the world are you doing this?"

He sighed and wished he could just go back to sleep.

"Doing what?"

"You know what I mean."

"I'm buying back what shouldn't have been sold. You thought selling this place and moving would fix us. How'd that work out for you?"

He'd been angry when his parents made the decision without talking it over with him. He'd been a kid in their eyes, a man in his own. After all these years he was righting their wrong. Maybe he shouldn't go that far in his accusations or explanation.

"Keeton, that isn't fair. You know why I had to get away from Dawson."

Yeah, memories. She'd been running from

memories. She'd said that everywhere she looked she saw something that reminded her of Kade. And most especially, she couldn't look at Sophie. She'd said looking at Sophie Cooper broke her heart. Everything had broken her heart. So she'd given up on family and buried herself in a job at the bank.

"Mom, selling out and moving didn't fix your family."

No need to remind her that his father, her ex-husband, now lived in subsidized housing and couldn't stay clean and sober for more than a month at a time. She'd taken a guy that had always been a rancher and turned him into a nine-to-five guy.

Would things have been better or worse if they'd stayed here?

No one would ever know the answer. But Keeton had a plan to bring his dad back here, to the land his parents and grandparents had owned. He wanted to give his dad the opportunity to be the person he'd been.

If he could just get back the land that had already been bought. Sophie's share didn't bother him. The biggest portion now belonged to a corporation. He meant to do some digging and find out who the owners were and what they planned on doing with it.

His mom reminded him she was on the other

end of the phone. He'd managed to push himself out of bed and limp across the room to the crib. Lucy slept soundly, her little cheeks pink and her thumb in her mouth.

Yeah, he guessed he should tell his mother she had a granddaughter. Deep breath, wait until she got finished with the lecture about buying the land and holding tight to the past.

"Mom, I have something to tell you."

"That you've come to your senses?"

He smiled at that. "No, I actually wanted to tell you that you're a grandmother."

"I'm what?" Her voice went quiet. "What?"

"Becka had a baby girl three months ago." Surprise! "I found out a few days ago when she brought Lucy and left her with me."

"She left her?"

"Yeah, seems a baby wasn't in her plans and she thought it would upset me to be saddled with my little girl." He smiled at the sleeping infant. "She couldn't have been more wrong."

"I'm a grandmother." His mom's voice softened by degrees and the land argument seemed to be forgotten. "I need to see her. When will you be back in Tulsa?"

"Not for a while. I guess if you want to see her anytime soon, you'll have to come to Dawson."

"That isn't fair."

"It's a town, Mom, nothing more."

"There are so many memories."

Hard things had to be said. He had to say it. "Mom, it's really time to move on."

"I have moved on. You're the one there buying land. You're the one still riding bulls."

"This land is about me moving on. And if you want to see Lucy, you have to come to Dawson."

"I'll see."

"I'd love for you to meet her." He walked out of the room, aware that his knee was still swollen and his back felt kinked in a few new places. Maybe he *was* getting old.

"I'll think about it."

"Good. I need to get off here and get ready for church."

"Okay." She didn't hang up, and he waited. "Check on your father. I usually talk to him a few times a week. I haven't been able to get hold of him this week."

They both knew what that meant. His mom asking him to check on his dad, though, that meant something, too. He'd have to think about that one.

"I will."

He dropped the phone onto the kitchen counter and wiped up water on the floor. It had rained last night and now he knew of another spot in the roof that needed fixed. He looked up at the old ceiling, spotted with brown. Some new leaks, and some old.

He put on the coffee and went to get ready for church.

When he walked out of the bathroom the mangy tomcat was sitting in the hall looking at him. "How'd you get in here?"

The cat mewed at him.

"I'm not feeding you more tuna."

He heard Lucy whimper and fuss. He walked down the hall to the bedroom. The old tabby followed. As he picked Lucy up he looked back at the cat, now sitting on his dresser. "Really, cat?"

The cat licked its paws, hopped down and followed him to the kitchen where Lucy's baby seat was on the table. Obviously the cat didn't get that Keeton had never been a cat person. As soon as he settled down he planned on getting a dog. A smart dog, like a border collie. Not a cat.

He opened another can of tuna and set it on the floor. Next he fixed a bottle and he poured himself a cup of coffee. With Lucy in one arm, the bottle cradled next to her body, he walked out the front door, holding his coffee in the opposite hand.

Yeah, not a bad life. A front porch of an old house, good coffee and a pretty sweet baby. He kicked back in a lawn chair he'd pulled out of the back of his truck and settled down to feed Lucy.

"Baby girl, I sure do love you."

She smiled up at him, cooing with the bottle in her mouth.

"And you aren't always going to love me. You'll have plenty of time to be mad at me and to think my rules are the worst. But I'm always going to love you." He kissed her forehead, and she was still warm.

"Tomorrow we're going to the doctor. I think three days of this virus is enough." To top it off, she'd started coughing during the night. It was a bad cough, sounded kind of like a horse that had just eaten dusty hay. He stood and carried her back inside. He needed a diaper bag, an extra bottle and his Bible.

As he walked out the front door a short time later, the mule of Lucky Cooper's ran across the road and through the ditch. Keeton grinned and shook his head. He'd made a plan yesterday for catching that mule.

But then he'd seen it next to Sophie's barn. And she'd been petting it while it ate from a bucket of grain. Lucky had been one-upped by his sister.

Sophie hadn't gone to church that morning. She'd woken up several times during the night feeling kind of creeped out. She didn't normally do things like that. She'd lived on her own a long time and usually didn't get scared. Especially in her house.

She'd bought the old stone house of the Browns several years ago. She had loved the front porch with the arched, stone columns. She loved the cool, shadowy interior of the rooms on the front of the house and the bright openness of the kitchen and family room. As a kid she used to ride by and dream about someday living in the stone house.

And last night, for the first time, she'd been afraid. She'd actually considered calling Dylan to come down and stay the night. If she did that, though, she'd never get past it. She'd be teased. And she would also fall in to the habit of calling her family every time she heard a noise.

She'd made it through the night, pepper spray on her bedside table. As she got up, she slipped the pepper spray into her purse. In case. She didn't know in case of what, but just in case.

At noon she walked out her front door dressed in a loose skirt and a tank top. She'd head right to her parents' for lunch. She'd even made a fruit salad to take along. She set it on the seat next to her and backed out of the garage. As she eased down the drive she saw a truck pull away. It had been parked on the shoulder of the road.

She sped up, trying to see who it might be. They hit the gas and left her behind. And she had no intentions of trying to catch the truck. Instead she watched it pull out of view as she turned onto the road to the Cooper ranch.

As she eased up the driveway, crossing Cooper Creek, she started to relax. Her calm was short-lived. The old blue truck parked next to Lucky's mammoth-size SUV meant that someone had deemed it necessary to invite Keeton West to Sunday lunch.

The cowboy Cupid was on the loose.

The front door of the house opened and Travis walked down the steps. He must have been waiting for her. The grin spreading across his face said it all. She would have to remind him that he didn't have seniority and as the older sister she could still do something about his smugness.

"Carry this." She handed him the fruit salad and pretended she hadn't noticed Keeton's truck.

"We have company."

"I know." She grabbed her purse and pushed the door closed. "Mom couldn't help herself."

Travis grinned. "Sorry, this time it wasn't Mom."

"Seriously?"

"Nope."

Not Mom. She glared at Travis and he didn't even look ashamed of himself. When had he ever? "Not you."

"Sorry."

"Traitor." She took back her fruit salad. "I have nothing more to say to you."

"'Thank you' would be nice."

"No, thanks." She marched ahead of him, knowing her behavior bordered on ridiculous but unsure of how to change it. She turned before going up the steps. "Trav, you know how I feel."

"I know what you've always said. And after last night…"

"No."

He shrugged and his big grin turned sheepish. "Sorry, but there aren't many people who didn't see."

The kiss.

She wanted to hide. She could leave right now and head back to her place. The fruit salad she'd made would feed her for a week.

"You might as well face the music," he offered as he stepped next to her. He wore one of his very rare serious expressions.

She ignored him and walked up the steps and through the front door. She didn't hide. She wouldn't hide. Instead she would do what her brother recommended and face her family. With her head held high she walked into the kitchen. Of course Keeton smiled as she walked through the door. Of course her family all turned and stared.

From the way they were acting, a person would think she never dated, never kissed a man.

She did date. She paused to think because she really couldn't remember the last time. Well, she had reasons. She worked a lot of hours. Most of the men her age were already married.

She set the salad on the counter and poured herself a cup of coffee. She was a Cooper. She knew how to deal with this bunch and their interference. She'd been dealing with it her entire life. Which was why she kept some things to herself.

With so many Coopers, secrets seemed almost impossible.

For several years when she had dated, she tended to meet her dates in town. It gave less opportunity for a family inquisition. So why in the world would she step into Keeton West's arms in a very public place?

"What can I do, Mom?" She walked up to her mother. Angie Cooper stirred a boiling pot of pasta and pointed to bread on a baking sheet.

"Get that in the oven for me. And then see if you can round someone up to fill glasses with ice."

"No problem." She hugged her mom before carrying out the orders. "Sorry I missed church. I didn't get a lot of sleep last night."

"I wonder why." Her mom smiled and went back to stirring.

Sophie would let her mom think she knew the

reason, even if it was embarrassing to allow that conclusion to be the one everyone came to. No way would she tell them the real reason and have them all worrying. If she told, she'd end up with guards on all corners of her house.

"Can I help?" A quiet voice behind her.

She turned and smiled at Keeton. He had Lucy in a pouch strapped over his shoulders and around his waist. She wanted to kiss the baby, but she didn't want to be that close to Keeton, so close she could almost feel him. His scent, clean soap and cologne, filled the air around them.

She stepped back.

"I'm good. Thank you."

"I can fill the glasses with ice." He held up his hands. "Two free hands thanks to your mom. She found this pouch in the closet."

"We do have a lot of baby stuff around here."

"So, ice?"

She pointed to the cabinet. "Glasses up there. You'll have to do a head count to see how many of us showed up today."

"Not a problem." He leaned in close. "You smell good."

"Go."

He laughed and walked away with an easy swagger and a definite limp. She shook her head and grabbed the baking sheet with the bread.

When he returned, she did reach in to touch

Lucy's cheek. Burning up. She used her wrist, thinking it might be her imagination. Or maybe the baby felt warmer because she was in the pouch and close to his body.

"Keeton, she's really warm."

"I just gave her a dose of fever reducer an hour ago."

That got Angie Cooper's attention. "If you gave it to her an hour ago, she shouldn't be burning up now."

"Where's Jesse?" Sophie looked around for her brother the doctor who sometimes managed a Sunday with the family.

"On duty." Lucky walked up, his attention on the tiny baby held close to Keeton's chest. "She looks kind of warm in there."

"No, that's heat from a fever." Angie pulled the baby from the pouch and held her close. "I think you need to take her to the E.R."

"I took her to the doctor the other day. They said she had a virus." Keeton looked from Sophie to her mom. "But I'm ready to take her if you think that's the best thing."

"I do." She held the baby close and fussed over her. "She's too quiet. Has she had a cough or any other symptoms?"

"She coughed a lot last night."

"You should definitely take her to the E.R." Angie snuggled Lucy close.

"Sophie can drive you." Trav tossed her the purse she'd hung over a chair at the table. She caught it but not because she planned on driving Keeton, but because if she didn't, it would hit her.

"I can drive myself. Sophie can stay and have lunch with her family." Keeton took the baby back from Sophie's mom.

Sophie watched and she knew what it might feel like to be a sinking ship. Her mom glanced from Keeton to her. Heather had moved close to examine the baby—and then to examine Sophie.

Sinking fast.

"I'll drive you." Sophie pulled her keys out of her pocket and held them up. "You can have that knee checked while we're there."

"My knee is fine." His voice was low, husky and a little tense. "I really can drive myself."

Yes, but he'd be dealing with a sick baby fussing, wanting attention. She didn't doubt him, she just knew it would take more than one person and she wouldn't want to do this alone.

"I'm going with you." Sophie hugged her mom. She blew a kiss to her dad who stood at the end of the counter watching, his hazel eyes taking everything in.

"You're sure?" Keeton had picked up the backpack he used as a diaper bag and he pulled out a bottle that he reached to hold under the faucet.

"I'm sure."

Keeton put a top on the bottle of water and shoved it in the backpack. He walked next to her as they went out the front door to her car.

For May it was really warm. The sky was summer blue, no haze. Sophie considered backing out. But how could she? She told herself he'd do the same for her.

Friends helped friends.

"I need to get her car seat." Keeton started for his truck, still cradling Lucy in his arms. "Do you want to hold her while I get it?"

"Of course." She took the baby and held her close. "She's really warm."

"Yeah. You know, I'm starting to think I'm not good at this dad business. I really thought the virus would run its course."

"How were you supposed to know it would linger?"

"And get worse." He had the car seat and followed her to the sedan. "I can drive."

"Not my car." She opened the back door for him to put the car seat in. "I'll drive."

"You don't give an inch, do you?" He straightened and she leaned in to buckle Lucy into the seat.

"Nope." She whispered to the baby girl, smiling at the tiny little face. "You'll be fine, sweetie."

"What if it's more than a virus?"

Sophie kissed Lucy on the cheek, and then she closed the car door and turned to face him. "She's fine."

Sophie tossed him her car keys, a concession because she knew he was nervous and driving the car happened to be something he could control at the moment. He looked like a man who needed to be in control.

"You think I'm obsessing, right?" He felt out of control. One tiny little girl had managed to undo his world, his calm, his life.

And then he'd been blindsided by Sophie Cooper and leftover feelings from years ago.

He moved the driver's side seat back and adjusted the steering wheel of her car. She had climbed in on the passenger side but she looked back at Lucy, glancing over her shoulder from time to time to make sure his daughter was okay.

For a brief moment he wondered where Becka might be and if she'd want to know that their daughter was sick. He doubted it since she hadn't left a way to get in touch with her. He'd talked to a lawyer and that seemed to be a point in his favor.

"I don't think you're obsessing," Sophie finally answered. "I think you're being a dad who cares about his daughter."

"Right." He turned on the left blinker and pulled onto the main road that would take them to Grove.

"I saw a truck parked in front of my house this morning." Her voice fell quiet in the car and she didn't look at him as she made the statement.

Keeton nearly stopped but he couldn't, not on a main road. Not with traffic traveling in both directions. "What do you mean, there was someone in front of your house?"

She shrugged and turned to look at him, her eyes shadowed. "I guess they're watching me."

"And you didn't tell your family. You waltzed in with a fruit salad like everything was a-okay."

"It is okay. I know how to shoot a gun. I have pepper spray."

"There's more to this than protecting yourself. You're being harassed and now you're being stalked. Soph, you can't ignore this."

"I'm not ignoring it. I'm telling you. Telling my family is…"

"Please don't say it's complicated."

She laughed a little but then her smile faded. "I wasn't going to say that. Okay, maybe I was. But you know my family. They'll take over. This is my project. This is my life."

"Right, so you don't want to be a Cooper?"

"I am a Cooper, but even a Cooper needs a life of her own."

"Gotcha."

He pulled up to the hospital and parked in the lot designated for the E.R. When they walked through the doors of the emergency room, cool air greeted them and a young woman smiled from behind her desk. The waiting room looked pretty empty. Maybe that meant there wouldn't be a long wait.

"Can I help you?" The receptionist smiled at Lucy, and then made eye contact with Sophie.

And Sophie looked at him, because she wasn't his little girl's mother. But she held her as if she could be.

They looked like a family. And he suddenly wanted that. More than he wanted land. More than he wanted a world title in bull riding.

"My daughter's had a virus and her fever isn't responding to the medicine the doctor told me to use."

They spent five minutes answering questions, filling out forms and then were escorted to a triage room where a nurse took Lucy's vitals and announced that her fever had shot up to 103.6.

"That's pretty high for a little girl." The nurse cuddled Lucy, now stripped down to just a diaper. "And some diarrhea, too?"

From the looks of that diaper, the answer to that would be a yes. The nurse handed Lucy to Sophie. And Sophie shot him a look. He shrugged and smiled at her. When he held out his arms to take Lucy, Sophie shook her head and reached for the diaper bag. She reached inside for a diaper and wipes and put Lucy on the exam table to change her.

"I'll give you a minute." The nurse slipped out of the room.

Keeton stepped back, kind of glad someone else had taken this one. He'd been changing them for two days. Even now, without looking, his stomach twisted a little. He'd seen a lot of disgusting things in his life and never thought he'd be the guy with the weak stomach, but diapers were a whole new ballgame.

"I should have let you change this." Sophie sniffed and turned her head away as she tossed the offending diaper in the plastic bag the nurse walked through the door with. "Blech."

Keeton picked up his daughter. Sophie moved to the sink to wash her hands.

"Thanks, Soph."

The nurse's eyes narrowed. "You're not the mom."

Sophie shook her head, drying her hands on a paper towel and then reaching for antibacterial lotion on the shelf. "No, just a friend of the father."

"Only a real friend would change a diaper

like that." The nurse laughed and picked up her clipboard. "If you'll follow me, we'll get you in a room and have a doctor in there as soon as possible."

Ten minutes later it was Jesse Alvarez Cooper who walked through the curtains that separated Lucy's cubicle from the others in the small E.R. He glanced up, looked at his clipboard and then shot his sister a look. "You have a baby?"

"Keeton's." She flared her nostrils at Jesse and pointed a finger at him. "Don't mess with me, little brother."

"Right." Jesse reached for Lucy and placed her on the bed. "Any difficulty breathing?"

He held a stethoscope to her chest and looked at Keeton as though he should have answers.

"Not that I've noticed. I know that your mom said to get her to the emergency room." Keeton watched as Jesse continued to examine his daughter. Lucy dozed a little in his arms.

Jesse held Lucy with ease and checked her ears and nose. "My mom would be the one to trust. Any coughing?"

Keeton could answer that with confidence. "Yeah, last night she coughed quite a bit."

"Hmm." He leaned the baby forward and placed the stethoscope on her back. "We'll get X-ray down here and get a picture of these lungs."

"What's wrong?" Keeton stood, ignoring Sophie's light squeeze on his arms.

"I think it's possible she has a light case of pneumonia. And she's definitely in need of some fluids. We'll get the X-ray and then move her to a room where she can rest. IV fluids and antibiotics, Keeton. She'll be fine in a few days."

"She's going to be okay?"

Jesse lifted Lucy and held her close. "She's going to be better than okay."

Keeton believed Jesse but it didn't feel so great, watching his baby girl go through X-rays, then having an IV attached to her little arm. She squirmed and cried a weak cry, wriggling in his arms as they pushed the needle in place. The nurse smiled a gentle smile and brushed fingers through Lucy's strawberry-blond curls.

"There we go. Now let's get her down to a room." The nurse in teddy-bear scrubs and soft-soled shoes smiled at them, easing them through the situation.

Keeton had kind of arrived late to the dad game, but this was what it was all about. Holding Lucy, walking down the hall with her in his arms, whispering that everything would be okay. He held his little girl close, because he had a lifetime of this, of keeping her safe.

The only thing not certain to be in his future

was the woman walking next to him. And the more time Sophie spent with him, the more he wanted her in his life.

Chapter Six

Sophie watched as Keeton dozed in a vinyl hospital recliner, his jean-clad legs stretched in front of him. The chair didn't quite match his cowboy frame and he had angled himself sideways. Lucy slept in his arms, a pillow propping her up. Her little hand touched his cheek and he moved, tilting his head closer to his daughter.

After a few minutes Keeton blinked and opened his eyes. "I thought you'd be gone."

"No, but I do need to leave pretty soon."

He sat up a little, still cradling Lucy in his arms. "I appreciate you coming with us."

"I'm glad I could be here." For the most part. And then a part of her knew she'd made a mistake. She kept walking further and further into his life. Her heart couldn't keep up. It needed gradual training, not diving right into all of this emotion.

Emotion was messy. It left marks. Scars. Lots of scars.

She stood up, holding her purse on her shoulder, unsure of how to make her exit without looking like a woman on the run. Keeton smiled, as if he knew. He didn't move from the recliner, not with his sleeping baby girl attached to an IV. Instead he winked.

"Sophie, I know you need to go. We'll be fine. But you might need to come back for us tomorrow."

"I can do that." Or get someone to do it for her.

"Will you?" His voice had a husky tone, sleepy and kind of sweet.

"I will." She stopped at the door. She considered kissing him goodbye. And then she didn't. He was clutter.

She enjoyed a neat, orderly life. She and her sister Heather were a lot alike in that area. They liked their personal space. They liked a certain amount of calm. It probably came from sharing a bedroom with Mia. Or Messy Mia, as they'd called her growing up.

Mia loved clutter. She loved loud music. She wanted to someday own a coffee shop.

Walking down the hall, her heels clicking on tile floors, Sophie relished that she had nothing in common with Mia. Chaos didn't suit her.

As she drove away from the hospital she wondered if that were true, about chaos and clutter. By starting this housing project, hadn't she cluttered her life a little? Maybe she'd needed something in her life to keep her from getting in the rut of sameness? Yes, at thirty-five she'd become a stodgy spinster. She went to her job at Cooper Properties at the same time every day. She ate the same lunch, fixed the same dinner. She'd had two cars in seven years, both the same, right down to the color. The only difference this time was that she'd splurged for satellite radio.

She'd started the housing project because a young woman in her office had mentioned wishing she could stay in Dawson but there weren't many rental houses and she couldn't afford to buy.

It didn't matter. The housing development and Keeton were two different things. Keeton reminded her too much of what she'd lost. The housing development gave her something of her own.

She turned on the radio to drown thoughts that bordered on chaos. As she drove along the quiet paved road toward her house she slowed to look in her rearview mirror. She could hear sirens, she just didn't know where they were coming from, but suddenly she saw smoke. Billowing smoke. Her heart raced ahead of her thoughts, because it came from the vicinity of her house. And the subdivision.

The sirens grew louder. She glanced in her mirror again, and then pulled to the side of the road so the fire truck could go around her. After a few minutes, to make sure nothing else might be coming down the road, she pulled out and followed the truck.

To Keeton's.

She pulled across from Keeton's burning home and parked. After a few minutes she got out of her car and stood, watching. Volunteers scurried, pulling hose, spraying, some watched.

The little house billowed and blazed. As she watched, it collapsed in on itself. The volunteer firemen from Dawson jumped back from the blaze but continued to spray a steady stream of water at the burning house. Smoke filled the air, acrid and thick, burning her nostrils.

As she watched from the edge of the drive, Jackson turned, saw her and raised a hand. He walked toward her in his gray-and-yellow suit. When he got close he pulled off his protective helmet and brushed a hand through his hair.

"It went fast." He swiped his arm across his perspiration-covered brow.

Smoke burned her eyes. She blinked to clear her vision and watched as the little house, so long a fixture in her memories, burned to the ground. "What happened?"

"From the looks of things, arson. We'll leave that up to the investigators, but I'd say the gas can we found tossed by the barn is a good indicator. They probably meant to torch the barn but maybe lost their nerve, or thought someone was coming."

"Who would want to burn his house down?" She choked the words out and her eyes watered from smoke, from sadness.

"Good question. Another one is, why? One of the guys said he saw a truck across the street messing around the houses being built. When he pulled over to see who it was, they took off. He said he hasn't seen that truck around here before."

"Was anything damaged over there?"

"You mean at the mystery subdivision." Jackson leaned against her car, smelling of smoke and perspiration.

"Yes, that's what I mean."

"Why would you care?"

"Because those are people's homes and lives. I care. And because I live just down the road."

"And you own that land?" Jackson smiled a tight smile as he pulled off the heavy fireproof jacket.

"Jackson."

"I'm not going to tell anyone." He leaned in again. "I'm curious, though. What are you up to, sis?"

"Do I have to share everything?"

"No, but sometimes it helps us to work things out if we share. We Coopers might interfere a lot, but we can be pretty helpful, too."

"I want to do this. I want to accomplish this on my own, without family coming to the rescue. I'm thirty-five. I need something of my own."

"I get that, but is it so bad, having us butting in?"

"It isn't bad, but it can be suffocating."

A police car eased up the driveway. Jackson waved at the officer, and then turned back to face her. Sophie had kind of hoped the arrival of the local deputy would be her out. Not so lucky.

"Go ahead with your project, Soph. But stay safe, and if there's something going on, you need to let me know."

"What about Keeton?"

He shrugged. "What about him? He isn't my problem. Is he yours?"

"No, but someone needs to tell him about his house. He'll need somewhere to go with the baby."

"I have it on good authority that he has a nice place on the outskirts of Broken Arrow. Why are you suddenly so concerned with Keeton West's welfare?"

"I'm not." Yes, she was. Jackson gave her a look that said he knew better.

"I suppose you know where he is?"

"At the hospital with his little girl."

"Then I guess you can be the one to tell him about his house." Jackson pulled his jacket and then the gloves back on. "Remember when you caught the bouquet at my wedding?"

"You're not funny. And I don't believe God plans our lives based on who catches a bouquet."

"I'm just having fun with you."

"Thanks, it was fun for me, too."

Jackson held his hat and glanced from the fire to her. Sophie shifted her focus to the remains of the house.

"Sophie, do me a favor and be careful. Call if you see anything unusual."

"I will." She sighed. "I guess I'll go give Keeton the news."

"I can do it later."

She shook her head and Jackson opened her car door. After a quick hug she climbed in and he closed the door behind her. She backed into a clearing and turned her car around.

When she got to the intersection she turned toward Grove and she thought about how to tell Keeton this news.

* * *

When Sophie had walked back into the hospital room just over an hour after leaving, Keeton had been pleased and then worried. She hadn't smiled as she walked through the door. Instead she'd told him something had happened and she was sorry. Tears had trickled down her cheeks and she'd wiped them away as she explained to him about his house.

He'd driven her car while she stayed with Lucy. As he'd pulled up the driveway, Jackson had stepped away from a group of men. He'd watched as Keeton got out of Sophie's car, and he hadn't said anything. Yet.

For now the two stood side by side looking at the charred, still-smoldering remains of the house. Keeton shook his head. Someone had burned his house to the ground. At least he'd been gone. Lucy hadn't been sleeping in the bed that had disappeared among the smoldering, blackened wood and siding. Even the cat had escaped. It was sitting on a fence post, licking its paws.

"This is crazy." He shook his head and walked around the smoldering heap of remains. "Who did this?"

"I don't know." Jackson walked up and stopped next to him.

Keeton turned from the house to Jackson. "Did anyone see anything?"

Jackson frowned and walked toward the porch where they thought the fire started. "A truck has been lurking around the area. Someone saw it parked in front of Sophie's this morning, early."

"Yeah, she mentioned that."

Jackson tossed the stick he'd been holding. The cat mewed and ran back to the barn. "And you didn't think her family should know?"

"Jackson, let me remind you of something, Sophie is a grown woman." Keeton took a step toward Jackson and kept his voice down. People were cleaning up the area and a few turned to watch. "I know you want to protect her. Do it. But don't think you have to protect her from me. And I'm pretty sure she doesn't want you to storm into her life, taking charge of something she thinks she has handled."

Jackson squared his shoulders, his jaw clenched. "Sophie knows how to put together a business deal, Keeton. She knows how to make a project run efficiently. She's never dealt with something like this."

"That's probably true, but I think if you try to tell her she doesn't know what she's doing, she might get a little upset with you."

"So how do you think we should handle this?"

Keeton turned to face what had been his future

but now lay in ashes. "I guess maybe involve her instead of taking over."

"Then you see what you can come up with. And in the meantime, you can move yourself into her guesthouse and keep an eye on her."

Keeton turned to face Jackson again. "What are you talking about?"

"You're planning to rebuild, right?"

"Of course I am."

"Sophie has a guesthouse above her garage. It was the old caretaker's apartment from when the garage was a carriage house."

"You want me to move into Sophie's guesthouse?"

"Seems like the perfect plan to me."

Jackson had to be losing his mind. Keeton thought about explaining that to him. But the fact that it didn't seem like a bad idea had him kind of convinced maybe he wasn't too far behind Jackson.

"I don't think I'm going to move myself onto Sophie's property, and then tell her we decided it was for the best."

"Chicken." Jackson grinned and then he laughed. He pounded Keeton on the back. "I always thought you had more guts than that. Maybe you're all show."

"I think there's more to it than that. I think she wouldn't appreciate us trying to take over. If you haven't noticed, Sophie really is able to take care of herself."

"Maybe so, but in this instance, her family is going to make sure she's safe."

Keeton had no intention of telling Jackson he might be clueless when it came to his sister. Then again, maybe someone needed to say something.

"I know you want to make sure she's safe but Sophie's been fighting you guys for freedom her whole life." And that's all he planned on saying. Let them figure it out the way he had, by talking to her.

"Fighting us how?"

"Jackson, she's building a subdivision and none of you knew."

Jackson pushed his hat back and turned to look across the road. A slow grin spread across his face and he laughed a little.

"Yeah, I guess you have a point. But for the time being, she needs someone on her side, keeping her safe. For whatever reason, she's allowed you closer than the rest of us."

"Because I let her change her own flat tires." Yeah, it sounded like a joke but he hoped Jackson got that he was serious.

Jackson shrugged it off. "I know she can change a flat."

"But would you let her?"

"No, she's my sister."

"That's my point."

Jackson stopped smiling and watched as they returned the hoses and other equipment to the trucks. "Keeton, this whole situation with those houses and now this fire, has me worried."

"Me, too," Keeton admitted.

"I think this land deal of hers has stirred some people up and I'm not sure why."

Keeton didn't know what to say. Sophie had asked him to keep her secret. He'd promised. But keeping secrets could only go so far if it meant keeping her in danger. For the time being, though, he'd keep his mouth shut. He'd let her deal with Jackson and the rest of the Coopers.

When he walked through the door of the hospital room twenty minutes later a smile was pulled from him, and he thought smiling would be the last thing he wanted to do. Sophie had curled up in the chair with Lucy. The two were awake. And Lucy had the prettiest baby smile on her face as she looked up at Sophie.

"How'd it go?" Sophie didn't look up at him. Lucy had a finger on Sophie's chin and cooed as if she had something important to say.

"Great." He took a few steps closer. "She looks better already."

A half of a day of antibiotics and fluids had brought big changes to his little girl. Keeton walked into the room and set containers of Chinese takeout on the table. Sophie looked up, her smile soft, the look in her eyes, soft.

"Keeton, I'm really sorry. That house meant a lot. I know you're not feeling good right now."

"Not great, but I'll survive. At least we weren't in the house."

"I doubt they wanted to hurt you. They seem to be more interested in scaring people."

"Yeah, we just have to figure out who *they* are."

"I think that means finding out who wanted that land and why. Who bought up the land around us and why?"

"I can do some searching on that." He sat down on the edge of the bed. "Soph, we need to talk about the note you got."

"It's in my purse."

"We should give it to the police."

Sophie leaned her head toward Lucy and played with the baby, ignoring him. He sat on the edge of the bed, waiting, watching. Maybe falling in love. He shook his head to clear those thoughts.

There had always been something about Sophie, something he couldn't shake. He'd beat himself up a lot for those feelings.

"Soph?"

After a few minutes of smiling and talking to his baby girl, Sophie looked up, her hazel eyes locking with his. "I'll tell someone. I had hoped it was just kids playing a prank. You know? I mean, really, what happens in Dawson that needs the police involved?"

"Even Dawson has its share of problems."

"I know." She kissed Lucy's cheek, and then stood and eased the baby into the crib. "Where are you going to stay?"

"I haven't decided." No way would he mention that guesthouse and Jackson's idea. "I can go home to Broken Arrow and hire a few of your construction friends to rebuild for me. Or maybe get a temporary trailer."

She pulled a blanket over Lucy and turned to reach for a bag from the Chinese restaurant. "I have a guesthouse."

The offer took him by surprise. She had a way of doing that. That had to be one of the things about her that drew him the most. She looked so in control all the time, and then she did surprising things that no one expected.

"Are you offering to move me into your life?" He smiled, and then realized the words had been all wrong. She smoothed her skirt and slipped her bare feet back into jewel-encrusted flip-flops.

"I'm offering you a place to stay."

"Got it." He reached for his food. "I might take you up on that."

"And I'm going to take the dinner you bought me and go home for now." She walked to the door, tall and slender, her pale blue skirt swishing around her ankles.

At the door she turned. He remembered what he'd told Jackson. Sophie could take care of herself.

"Keeton, I'm not inviting you into my life. I care about you, and about Lucy, but…"

"I know." He wouldn't make her say it. She had loved his brother a long time ago. Maybe she didn't want the memories. Maybe it was about bull riding.

Either way, he got it. And he didn't accept it. But he wasn't about to tell her, not yet.

Instead he planned to show her what she didn't seem to be accepting. She had a past. But the two of them could have a future. He'd felt it when he held her. And he kind of thought she had, too. He guessed those mammoth walls she'd built around herself were the one thing keeping him out of her life. Just call him Joshua because those walls of hers were coming down.

Chapter Seven

A few days after the fire at Keeton's, Sophie watched the men working on the Tillers' house. The frame was up. Jana Tiller stood nearby, her smile hesitant, as if she feared the dream of owning this house, this land. Sophie ignored the second phone call from Keeton, who had gone to Tulsa on business the day after the fire. He'd explained something about his property in Broken Arrow and a meeting with Hightree, Inc.

She'd thank him later for the cat he'd moved to her place.

The calls weren't about the cat. She knew he'd want to talk about giving the letter to the police. She'd already done what he asked, and they'd thanked her and shoved it in the bag with other evidence collected, because they didn't see how it could be connected to Keeton's house. End of story. She hoped.

"What next?" Gabe walked up behind her, making her jump a little. She liked him, but he had a way of watching her that creeped her out a little. But he had volunteered to help build houses while he drew unemployment from his welding job. That made him a great friend to the Tillers and to others who were building. She could excuse his immaturity and serious lack of social skills because he had a good heart.

"I think you'll have to ask Jason. He's in charge of 'what next.'" She smiled and nodded in the direction of Jason Kent. "Right over there."

"Yeah, I'll ask. I need to head out for a few hours. I have a job to interview for."

"That's great." Her phone rang again. She answered it this time. "Sophie Cooper."

"I just saw your new houseguest driving through town with a loaded-down truck. Thought I'd warn you that he's heading your way."

"Thanks, Jackson, I really appreciate you interfering in my life." She smiled at Jackson's uneasy throat clearing on the other end of the phone and she walked away from the crew. The people standing nearby were suddenly talking a little quieter and looking her way.

"I knew you'd enjoy having someone close by."

"Of course."

He paused and the radio volume turned down

in his truck. "On a serious note, I do think we'll all sleep a little better if he's over there."

"Right, and this isn't about interfering in my life?"

He laughed. "Yeah, it's all about that."

"Thanks for admitting it."

"You're welcome. When you heading home?"

"Pretty soon. I had a full day at the office and it looks like things are going pretty good here." She glanced at her watch and at the crew that had gone back to work. Jason was showing the Tillers a few things they could work on. They were all learning the steps of building a house.

"Hey, Soph." Jackson cleared his throat. Time for the other shoe to drop. "Watch for things that seem unusual. Don't be afraid to call the police."

The air got a little heavy and her arms tingled. Sophie turned to face the people standing near the house, all ignoring her now.

"Yeah, I'll be careful."

She said goodbye and slipped the phone back into her purse. All of her life she'd lived in Dawson. All of her life she'd taken for granted that her community was safe, her neighbors were her friends. Something had changed. She shivered a little as she looked at the house frame, because it had something to do with this land and these houses. Doing something good for people shouldn't put everyone she cared about in danger.

After making her rounds and saying good-bye, Sophie walked to her truck and made the short trip back to her house. She smiled as she pulled into the drive and parked, not because of the truck parked near the garage, but because that silly mule stood near the barn waiting for his nightly ration of grain. One of these days she'd tell Lucky that his mule had taken up residence at her place. She might even tell him she'd had a bridle on said mule and had leaned across the animal's back.

As she walked up the steps to her front porch she glanced back at the garage and the upstairs guesthouse. No signs of life. She slipped the key in her front door and stepped inside.

It felt good to be home. She loved the quiet, cozy feel of her house. She'd had her sister Heather decorate, and the home had a bungalow decor with overstuffed chairs, braided rugs on the hardwood floors and the occasional antique piece of furniture to bring it all together. Her house. Her space.

She kicked off the high heels that had kept her toes cramped all day and walked through the arched door of the kitchen. The coffeepot did its thing. Five o'clock and it started to brew. She smiled as she walked through to the laundry room and found her favorite sweats and her tie-dyed T-shirt. Comfy clothes, a cup of coffee and something easy for dinner.

After changing she poured her coffee and opened the cabinets to see what looked good. Peanut butter, toaster pastries, cereal. She reached for a box of cookies and realized that wouldn't really qualify as a meal, not even with milk. But why not? She was thirty-five years old. If she wanted cookies for dinner, she could have cookies.

Or a grilled PB and J, with blackberry jam, of course. Buttered, grilled to perfection, the peanut butter melting into the jam on the inside. She reached for the loaf of bread on top of the microwave and frowned at the green growing inside. So much for her sandwich.

Plan two. She turned on the radio and eighties music blasted. Why did eighties soundtracks make a person want to slide across the kitchen floor—even a person in her thirties—and drink milk from the carton?

Milk and cookies, the dinner of champions.

She paused as she lifted the milk jug and listened. She'd heard something. Or maybe not. A faint sound, a click, a thump?

Keeton walked up the steps to Sophie's back porch. She'd gotten home fifteen minutes earlier. He'd waited, thinking she'd come over, see if they'd gotten settled. Then he realized she wouldn't. Because he knew Sophie and she'd be thinking and rethinking the decision she'd made, and regretting.

He stopped at the back door and smiled as he peeked through the window. Sophie Cooper never ceased to amaze him. Eighties rock blasted from a poor-quality radio and Sophie had just lifted a jug of milk to her lips. She drank from the carton? Sophie?

Lucy let out a little cry, announcing his presence. Sophie turned with a slight jump, paled a little and then frowned. She put the milk back in the fridge, turned down the radio and walked to the back door.

"Didn't mean to scare you. Or interrupt." He smiled, holding a much squirmier Lucy in his arms. Fluids and antibiotics had helped to produce a brand-new baby, nothing like the quiet little girl he'd been handed by Becka.

"You didn't." She smiled at Lucy and the baby held her arms out. Just in time for his phone to ring.

He gave Sophie an apologetic smile that she shrugged off as she took his daughter.

"Answer it, I'll play with Lucy." She walked back inside and the door closed behind her.

"Sure, okay." Keeton watched her go and then answered his phone. It was Becka. He'd actually almost convinced himself she would leave them alone, that he'd never hear from her again.

Wishful thinking? But then, someday Lucy might want to see her mom.

"How's my baby?" When she started with those words, he knew he had trouble coming his way.

"She's good, Becka. She's great, actually." He leaned against the wooden rail of the back porch. He'd thought about how much to tell. How much to withhold. Withholding would make everything easier for him. "I'm having legal custody paperwork drawn up. I'll need an address so I can send you a copy."

"What do you mean, legal custody?"

Close eyes, count to ten, be patient. He opened his eyes and glanced toward the barn. The mule had stepped up to the water trough and lowered his head for a long drink.

"Becka, you left. You told me you didn't plan on being a mom. I thought that meant you were handing Lucy over to me. As a matter of fact, I know that's what you meant and I'm not going to play games with you. A child needs stability, not games."

"I'm not giving you my address."

"Abandonment suits me just fine."

"I didn't abandon her. I gave her to you. You're her dad."

"Right, and thank you. I love her and I plan on making sure she has a stable, loving home."

She hung up on him. It took a few minutes for his blood pressure to drop to a normal level. He leaned against the rail and thought about this life, the life he hadn't planned. Inside the house he could hear Sophie singing off-key to his daughter. Sophie, also not a dream he'd planned. But things changed.

He rapped on the door and walked inside. Sophie danced around the kitchen with Lucy and he really thought he heard his daughter laugh. Sophie heard it, too. She turned and smiled at him, one of those smiles that makes a person's face light up.

New dreams. What did he have to lose? He'd been drifting on the same path for years, not really risking anything. Why not take a chance on a new dream? Risk everything. He stopped at the edge of the counter and wondered how hard that would be, to give up old dreams for new ones.

He'd already sunk most of his money into land that now included a burned-out shell of a house.

What would Sophie say, if he asked her to take a chance with him? He thought maybe the time wasn't quite right to ask her. She was still adjusting to him in her life.

"I came to see if you had anything to eat." He

did his best to smile an easy smile. "I haven't been to the store."

She kissed the top of Lucy's head, "Did I see that mangy cat of yours sitting next to my garage?"

"I couldn't leave him behind."

"No, I guess you couldn't. I've been feeding him when I feed my barn cats."

"Thanks." He nodded in the direction of the coffeepot. "Mind if I have a cup?"

"Help yourself." She opened a cabinet. "And here are your choices for dinner. Yogurt in the fridge if you want healthy. I have cereal, toaster pastries. Um, the bread is moldy so PB and J is out."

"Do you have real food?"

She wrinkled her nose at the question and shook her head.

"I guess it depends on your idea of real food. I think I might have frozen pizzas in the freezer."

He guessed he didn't really know Sophie Cooper. He would have guessed her to be classical, not eighties, and salad, not cereal. "I'll check the freezer."

She mumbled something about him helping himself to her life. He grinned as he walked away from her. She had no idea just how true that statement would prove to be. He planned on being in her life for a very long time.

He opened the freezer door. "Hey, you have steak in here."

"Mmm-hmm. Yeah, Jackson always keeps me supplied with beef. I use some and take the rest to the food pantry in Grove."

"And then you eat cereal."

"Don't knock it." She peeked over his shoulder, pointing to the third shelf of the freezer. "See, frozen pizza."

"You're thirty-five and you eat like a college kid counting your quarters until payday."

"Sorry."

He turned, holding a package of steak, and she stood close, holding Lucy. He didn't kiss her. It wasn't easy, using that self-control, but he had a feeling she needed space and time to adjust.

"Do you have a grill?"

She pointed to the patio and the most amazing grill he'd ever seen. It looked as if it had never been used. "Go for it. You can thaw those out in the microwave. I think I have frozen French fries in there."

He opened the freezer and pulled out a full bag of fries.

"Dinner will be done in an hour." He stepped past her and Lucy reached, her little hands touching his arm.

He kissed his daughter's cheek before stepping

away to put the meat in the microwave to thaw. Yeah, new dreams and a new life.

While he got the steaks thawed and sprinkled them with seasoning from her sparse cabinet, Sophie hauled a playpen out of a closet, dragging it with her free hand and holding Lucy in the other arm.

"Let me help." He moved away from the counter, reaching for the playpen.

"I can do it. I have nieces and nephews, and I've taken care of plenty of babies."

Of course she had. She should have had her own kids by now. He followed her out the door, itching to take the playpen but knowing she'd rather just do it herself. That's the way she was wired. He remembered driving up behind her one night twenty years ago. Her old truck had broken down on the side of the road and she'd climbed up on the bumper, practically inside, to fix the thing.

He'd caught her smacking something with a wrench and asked if he could do it for her. She'd turned, dark hair framing a pixie face and hazel eyes shooting more sparks than her truck engine.

She'd told him that she could do it herself. And she had. That might have been the moment he'd fallen in love, come to think of it. Or at least developed a pretty healthy crush on her. A year later the crush had turned into huge guilt.

As she set up the playpen, he got the grill going. She handed Lucy over while she finished up, putting a blanket in the bottom for his daughter to lie on. Lucy loved the playpen. She could stretch out, squirm around. And there were gizmos that made noise.

"I don't have a clue what all she needs." He leaned over, smiling at his baby girl.

"You'll figure it out."

"So you're not going to offer to write up a list?"

She wrinkled that perky nose of hers at him and shook her head. "If you want me to."

"I'll manage." He opened the lid of the grill and placed the meat on the fire. "How do you want it cooked?"

"Medium." She opened a lawn chair and sat down.

When he turned she had a computer open on her lap. "What are you doing, checking status updates?"

She frowned and didn't look up. "I don't do social networks. I'm looking up who has bought land around here."

"Why do you think it's someone who bought land?"

"I don't know, it's just a hunch. Someone wants us both gone. It can't be about a subdivision. Your old farm isn't a subdivision."

"True." He sat down next to her.

"Maybe someone else wanted to build on that land. Maybe someone is thinking there is more oil to be had."

"That would be held up in the mineral-rights clause of a deed, wouldn't it?"

"Depends." She sighed and closed the computer. "That LLC is all I'm finding. I'll have to do more digging to find out who is involved with it."

He stood to check the steaks. "Did I see asparagus in your freezer?"

"Yeah." She leaned to talk to Lucy in soft baby talk. "Do you ever go to his grave?"

He hadn't expected that. But it was the link they shared. His little brother, losing him. "Once in a while, when I'm driving through."

"I can't." She sighed and looked up, shrugging slim shoulders.

"My parents haven't gone. I think they should. It's been a long time."

"I know. I think we all just had a hard time accepting that he was..." She brushed at her eyes. "I'm thirty-five. I've dated. I haven't really missed him in a long time and sometimes I feel guilty about that."

"It's okay that you went on with life, Soph. That's what people do. They hurt, they get angry, they mourn, they heal." He put the lid down on the grill and took a chair next to the one she'd sat in. "Sometimes they feel guilty."

Sophie reached for his hand. "You pulled the bull rope because he asked you to."

"I know." He brushed a hand through his hair and tried to find the right words. "I miss having a brother."

She nodded and didn't say anything. He knew that kind of silence, the kind that meant a person was working hard to hold it together, to not cry. He squeezed her hand and she squeezed back.

When she spoke her voice held a lingering softness. "I have a good life, Keeton. Sometimes I think about what might have been, but usually I'm okay. I have work and family, my church. Sometimes I really do go out on dates."

Yeah, he didn't really want to think about her dating. He let go of her hand and stood up, the pretense of checking the steaks making it a lot easier.

"I know."

The conversation was probably long overdue. His family had moved within six months of losing Kade. He'd gone to college in Tulsa. She'd gone to Oklahoma City. Still, it wasn't an easy conversation to have. The how-are-you-doing questions should have happened years ago.

When he turned from the grill she had a faraway look on her face, staring out at the field, smiling a little. He thought about holding her, about complicating things a whole lot for both of them. But now wasn't the time. He was a man and he wasn't totally clueless.

"I wonder how things would have been different if your parents had stayed."

"My dad wouldn't be an alcoholic."

"You want the land to bring him back here, don't you?"

He flipped the steaks again. "Yeah."

Silence. For a long time it was the two of them, cicadas in the trees, Lucy talking soft baby talk and cows in the field. After a few minutes Sophie stood and moved to his side. "You can buy the land, the hundred acres that I bought. I don't need it."

"It isn't that important. I have the twenty. My cash flow is going to be tight until my next payment from Jeremy."

"I'll hold it for you."

"Sophie, the land isn't that important. It won't fix everything. It won't force my mom to let go of her anger with Dad, with bull riding, with Dawson. She's moved on, I guess. Unless you bring up Dad and Dawson."

"Just the same, when you're ready, you can buy it."

He tucked a strand of hair behind her ear and his fingers remained but slid to her neck, felt her pulse flutter. She inhaled a soft breath and stepped back. "Sophie…"

She shook her head. "I'll get the fries and that asparagus."

And she hurried away, up the back steps and into the house, the screen door banging softly behind her.

They could try to fool themselves into thinking they were stuck in the past. He had news for her. This was very much about the present. And the future.

Tonight, though, it had to be nothing more than steaks on the grill and old friends spending time together.

Chapter Eight

Friday, the last day of May, the weather turned hot. Really hot. Sophie drove up to the barn at her parents' place late in the afternoon with the sun beating down. Of course Keeton's truck was parked in the driveway, next to Jackson's and Lucky's. She'd been thinking all day that this might be a hijacking—them inviting her here. They wanted something.

She had been given the role of purse holder for the Cooper brothers. Sometimes they ganged up on her to get what they wanted.

She happened to be very good at saying no. To show them she meant business, she'd put on a dress suit for this occasion. Her hair was back in a clip. She'd worn glasses instead of contacts. She smiled at the outfit, because she wore it when she needed to show that she had backbone and couldn't be sweet-talked.

As she walked through the double doors of the barn she could hear their voices, laughing and shouting over music that blared from the office. Lucky's wife, Anna, walked out of a stall carrying a brush. She clicked the door in place behind her and a dark gray head appeared. Anna petted the horse and smiled at Sophie.

"You ready to face three of them?" Anna rubbed the horse's head one last time and walked next to Sophie.

"I'm always ready for a fight." Sophie stopped walking, so did Anna. "I take it you know what they're after?"

"Oh, yeah, I know."

"So it's big?"

Anna peeked around the corner, in the direction of the doors that led to the arena. "Yeah, big."

"What is it?"

"They want Cooper Ranch to sponsor a bull ride. I can't remember which venue, but big."

"Why?"

Anna stopped talking and her smile faded. "I'll let them tell you. Hey, Soph, don't let them get to you."

"I won't." She gave her sister-in-law a quick hug, and then walked through the barn into the arena, stopping at the metal gate. The guys were standing at the chutes. No sign of Lucy. She had a feeling her mom was probably babysitting. Angie Cooper loved babies. Actually, she loved kids of all shapes and sizes. At the moment she even had two foster children.

Lucky ran a bull into a chute and Keeton prepared himself for a practice ride. Of course he wanted to stay in shape. He had events coming up that he would want to make, and win. Bull riding wasn't all about just showing up. These guys stayed in shape, they rode practice bulls and went to smaller events.

He settled on the back of the bull.

She wanted to turn away, to not watch. But she stood her ground. Years had passed since Kade. She could barely remember his laugh, his voice. She no longer felt that sick tug at her heart when she remembered. Sometimes she just felt alone. That had nothing to do with missing Kade, a boy she had thought she loved. She had loved him.

A long time ago. Bittersweet memories edged in and she even smiled, remembering. But today Keeton sat on the bull and Jackson stood next to him. Keeton, a man, not a boy. Life had changed them all. They'd grown up.

She smiled at the good memories—trail rides, pickup trucks, bonfires and rodeos. As she sifted the memories, Keeton somehow managed to be in every picture that clicked through her mind.

Jackson pulled the bull rope straight up, tight.

Keeton took it from him and wrapped it around his riding hand. The bull jumped, front legs coming up. Lucky pulled Keeton out of danger, holding him up until the bull settled again.

Time ticked away. Sophie concentrated on breathing, on staying strong. Keeton lowered himself onto the bull again and rewrapped his hand. He nodded. Travis, standing in the arena, opened the chute.

The bull spun from the small enclosure. Keeton moved with the jumps, the spins. His head tucked, his free arm helping to keep his balance. The bull lost the battle and Keeton made it to the buzzer. Eight seconds. The longest eight seconds in history.

She swallowed and fear slid down her throat, lodging on the lump that had built up as she'd watched. Keeton jumped from the bull. Travis kept the animal's attention as Keeton ran to the gate with a limp. He turned, saw her, nodded. He didn't smile. He knew better.

They wanted her permission to sponsor a bull ride.

Why should she care? What did she care about bull riding, about Keeton on the back of a bull? It didn't, shouldn't matter. Jackson yelled for her to join them. He smiled and waved. She saw the caution in his expression. Jackson always knew.

He'd been the person she confided in after

Kade's death. After his funeral. Jackson knew everything. Her heart paused and she reconsidered. Jackson knew *almost* everything.

Sophie walked around the outside edge of the arena and joined her brothers behind the chutes. And Keeton. He tipped his hat and he didn't smile. She lowered her gaze to his knee and the brace he wore to ride. She watched as he made easy moves, protecting his injured leg, and she wanted to call him names.

"So, Jackson, what brings me to the arena today?"

Jackson pointed to the risers that had been installed for the occasional competition that included spectators. Sophie led the way, the four men following. When she turned they all stopped, nearly running into one another. She hid her smile and took the last few steps to sit down.

"Tell me."

Jackson cleared his throat and took off his hat. She did laugh this time. They were ridiculous, four grown men in dusty boots and cowboy hats, faded jeans and button-up shirts, standing in front of her, scared silly.

Score one for the power suit. She smiled at them.

"We want to sponsor an event." Jackson sat down next to her.

She had the power. And yet she didn't. They knew how to work her. She smiled at the thought. They'd always known, her brothers. As kids if they'd wanted cookies, they'd managed to convince her it was somehow in her best interest to bake cookies. When they'd gotten in trouble as teenagers she'd gone to their father. She was the family diplomat.

And then she'd become the person who held them accountable with ranch funds. Because with this many men in a family, someone had to hold them accountable. Not that they weren't all quite capable. They each had their own interests, their own businesses, their own incomes. It was only with family funding for the bull operation that she kept track. Sometimes she wished she could rethink the master's in business and minor in accounting that had put her in this position.

"What kind of event?"

Lucky stepped forward and sat down next to her. "Let's stop playing games. Obviously Anna caught you before you came in here."

She shrugged. "Okay. And?"

"We want to sponsor an event that will raise funds for injured riders and their families."

Her heart trembled. "Oh."

Of course she couldn't say no. "When?"

"October. In Tulsa."

She nodded once. "Okay. Let me know what you need."

Keeton stepped forward, his mouth open to say something. She didn't want to look at him, not in those orange chaps and dusty cowboy hat. Her heart couldn't take looking at him. But then his phone rang and he had everyone's attention.

"Mom?"

The conversation continued in nods and sighs and softly spoken words. He walked away. Jackson looked from Keeton to Sophie. "That doesn't sound good."

"No, it doesn't." She watched Keeton stand by himself. She thought he'd done that too often. He'd taken care of his parents. Whom had he turned to while his family fell apart? His grandparents had both been gone by then. Maybe he'd still had his mom's family in Tulsa. Sophie didn't know.

He put the phone back in his shirt pocket and took off his hat to rake a hand through short, dark hair. As he walked back he unbuckled the chaps and when he got to them he reached down to pull off his spurs.

"Dad's in the hospital in Tulsa." He piled chaps and spurs with his bull rope on the bleachers.

"I'm sorry. What happened?" Sophie asked, making room for him to sit next to her. He shook his head and continued to stand.

"Drinking and driving. Fortunately he was alone and no other cars were involved. I need to get Lucy and head that way."

"I'll go with you." Sophie stood and then she rethought her offer. But it was already out there and he looked relieved. Maybe because he'd handled too much alone in his life. She'd always had her family, her very strong family with strong faith.

"You don't have to."

"I'm going with you. We can take Lucy. Or maybe leave her with Mom if you feel comfortable with that."

He nodded and reached for the equipment he'd piled on the bleachers. Jackson picked it up first. "Go, I'll take care of this."

Keeton nodded and thanked him.

An hour later they were heading fast toward Tulsa, and Sophie hadn't really had a chance to think about what she'd done. Other than to know she had never been this person, the impulsive one who didn't take time to think things through.

She'd made enough impulsive decisions in the last two weeks to last a lifetime.

Keeton glanced at the woman sitting in the passenger side of his truck. Angie Cooper had kept Lucy, so it was just Keeton and Sophie. She hadn't said much since they left Dawson. He figured she had a strong case of doubt and had been lecturing herself real good for hopping in this truck with him.

"Thanks for going with me."

She turned to smile at him. "You needed a friend."

"Yeah, I did. But I could have done this alone. He's going to be fine. It could have been worse."

"Keeton, your dad was in an accident. That is never easy to hear."

She had a point. They drove on and soon were easing through early evening traffic coming into Tulsa. Rush hour. Great. He checked his rearview mirror and got in the lane to take a right turn.

"I don't miss this traffic." He didn't miss living in the city. "You went to college in Oklahoma City, right?"

"Yes. What about you?"

"Here." He had a teaching degree he'd never used, but he'd always thought he'd be an agriculture instructor someday. He'd minored in marketing. That side of his degree came in handy when he'd gone into business with Jeremy Hightree.

They were quiet until he parked at the hospital and they were riding up to the third floor on the elevator. Sophie broke the silence. "When was the last time you saw him?"

"Six months."

The expression on her face told him that she'd never gone six months without seeing her parents. But she'd lived a different life, with different parents. Her parents had met their hard times head-on and survived. His family had fallen apart, walked away from their lives, their faith, one another.

Sometimes he wondered why. What made people of faith react in totally different ways? Was it the strength of their foundation? He'd seen it in houses after a tornado. Two houses, side-by-side. One would still be standing, the other would be flattened. The strength of the foundation, the way it had been framed, all of it made a difference.

He needed to remember that, to keep his faith strong. Storms had a way of coming back around again.

"Is your mom here?" Sophie asked the question as they stepped off the elevator. A natural question, he guessed. Neither of his parents had remarried but they didn't seem too interested in rekindling their own broken relationship. He doubted if they saw each other very often.

He was pretty surprised that his mom had known about the accident before he had.

"I doubt if she's here." He reached for Sophie's hand, kind of hoping the questions would end.

But maybe questions were easier than dealing with the hospital.

They walked down the hall to the room number his mother had given. He peeked in. His dad looked up from the bed and raised a hand in greeting.

"Is this what it takes to get you to visit?" James West waved them into the room as if nothing had happened. Keeton sighed and Sophie's hand tightened on his.

"I'd rather see you at home." Keeton pulled two chairs close to the bed for himself and Sophie. "What happened?"

His dad looked away. The curtains were open and the view of Tulsa as the sun set couldn't be beat, not even from a hospital room. Oklahoma had some of the prettiest sunsets. Keeton knew because he'd seen the sunset from coast to coast. There was something about this flat land that made the sun glow as it sunk over the western horizon.

"Look at those colors," James whispered, still avoiding honest discussion. Yeah, they'd been doing that for a long time. If there was one thing his family had become experts at, it was avoidance.

"Yeah, I'm glad you lived to see it."

Sophie's mouth opened and she gave him a narrow-eyed look. She didn't say anything.

Keeton rubbed a hand over his face and let out a sigh. Start over, be nice.

"You going to be okay?"

His dad turned from the window. "Yeah, I'm fine. I banged up my ankle."

"Good, glad you weren't hurt bad. What about the police?"

"Second strike. I'm not out yet."

"Is that what you're going for, Dad? Do you want to be out?" Anger had again sneaked back into his voice. "I'm sorry."

He had other things, harsher things to say, but it wasn't the time or the place. He removed his hand from Sophie's and leaned to look at his dad.

"I want you to come home with me. To Dawson."

"What are we going to do in Dawson, remember the good ol' days?"

"No, we're going to rebuild a farm and a legacy."

His dad turned to look out the window again. His chest rose and fell, his hand came up to wipe at his eyes. "I don't know if I can do it."

"Farm, or be sober?"

"Both, I guess." His dad sat up in the bed, repositioning his injured foot. "I'd sure like to be the man I was twenty years ago."

"I'll help you find him, Dad." Keeton felt the heat of emotion slice through his chest. He ducked his head and drew in a deep breath. "We'll do this together."

"Do what together?" The voice, clearly angry, came from the doorway.

Keeton turned, smiling at his mother. She'd obviously just gotten off work. She was a loan officer at a bank, had been for years. She and his dad had taken different turns after Kade died. His dad had found comfort in the bottle. Keeton's mom had buried herself in work and had ignored her pain and her family.

"We're moving back to Dawson." Keeton's dad said it with a smug smile. "I guess you made me sell the place, but you couldn't stop Keeton from buying it back."

"I know what he did." His mom walked into the room, her eyes going soft as she looked at Keeton's dad. Her lips pursed. "Are you okay?"

"Broken ankle. It's nothing. Remember when I fell off that rank colt, Doris?"

She didn't smile. "Yeah, you broke your fool back. I can't stay, but I wanted to check on you."

Keeton watched as his mom walked up to the bed. She rested a hand on his dad's shoulder and then she leaned and kissed his cheek.

"Thanks, Dor. I sure have missed you."

"Take care of yourself." She turned to Keeton and Sophie, as if she'd just remembered the two of them were sitting there. "Sophie, you look beautiful. I didn't expect to see you here."

There were words unspoken. Keeton guessed she wanted to add something like, "With Keeton."

"Thank you, Doris." Sophie stood to hug his mom. "Keeton got the phone call while he was at our place. I offered to come with him."

"That was sweet of you. You take care, okay?" His mom used a light, breezy tone. Avoidance had become a real art in the West family.

"I will. Hopefully we'll get to see you soon." Sophie dropped her hand from his mom's arm and took a step back.

His mom nodded and walked to the door. She stopped and turned to look at his dad in the bed. "I'll drive down to Dawson and check on you."

"Thanks, Dor. I appreciate that."

And then she left. Keeton sat there for a long time, thinking about his mom's change of heart until his dad drifted off. He stood then, easing himself up because his knee had gotten stiff sitting so long.

"Dad, we're going to take off. I'll be back tomorrow to take you home."

His dad opened his eyes a crack. "You got a home for us down there."

Keeton didn't know how to answer that. He'd had a home. Now he didn't. He hadn't really thought through what to do with his dad.

"He's staying in my guesthouse," Sophie answered for him. "There's plenty of room for you to stay with him, if you can handle the stairs."

He smiled at them. "Sophie, I'm an old pro at crutches and broken bones. I used to ride saddle broncs back in the day."

An old cowboy, that was Keeton's dad. And when you took a cowboy off the farm and handed him a sedan instead of a horse, something changed inside him. And it changed more when he saw a son put to rest long before his time.

"We should go." He touched his dad's arm. "Tomorrow."

"Thanks, Keeton."

They walked down the hall in silence. At the waiting room, empty at that late hour, Sophie stopped. He gave her a questioning look and she didn't respond with words. She pushed the door open and led him inside. The tiny room had a TV and two vinyl sofas. It was dark outside and the room was stuffy.

"You okay?" She stood close, still holding his hand.

He'd asked her the same thing years ago. She'd held his hand. He'd held her. He let go of that memory. They were no longer those two kids, adrift, lost. They were adults who had lived a lot and learned things about themselves.

They were learning more about each other. What could have been? Or maybe those thoughts were his alone.

"I'm good," he finally answered.

When she didn't move away, he stepped close and cupped her cheeks in his hands. She didn't protest, instead she closed her eyes and nodded once, giving him permission. Keeton kissed her because he needed to feel grounded. He needed to know that someone understood his heart. His fear. All of the things a man didn't want to admit to, he wanted to know someone got it without the words being said.

And the person who got him, who had always gotten him, was in his arms. He sighed into the kiss and she kissed him back. Her hands moved from her sides to his waist.

The door opened and he pulled back, laughing a shaky laugh as a nurse apologized and let the door close.

He touched his forehead to hers and whispered, "Thank you. I feel wrung out."

"I know." She was still holding him. "But maybe this is the beginning of healing for your parents."

"Maybe it is. It would be a long time coming."

"I know."

He wanted to ask her when healing started for her. Instead he held her again. Just held her.

"We should go." She whispered the words into his shoulder.

He didn't want to go. He wanted to hold her, to feel this connection for a long time. Instead he let go and stepped away.

"Yeah, it's a long drive." He opened the door. "And we haven't had dinner."

"We can hit a drive-through."

Right, time to bring this day to an end. He got it. He could always tell when she was backing away, ducking back into her shell. What she didn't know was that he had the faith to bring down walls.

Chapter Nine

James West sat in a lawn chair next to Sophie's garage. That mangy cat of Keeton's was curled up in his lap. Sophie parked her car in the driveway because the old farm truck she used for the housing development was in the garage. As she got out of the car she caught a glimpse of Lucky's mule. She smiled as the animal jumped the fence and ran off into the field.

"Hey, James." She pulled up a lawn chair and sat down next to Keeton's dad. "Do you need anything?"

He straightened his leg and shrugged. "Nah, I'm doing just fine. Keeton helped me down here when he left to go meet with someone about bulldozing the remains of my folks' old house. I can't believe someone burned that place."

"I know. It's a huge loss to Keeton, too."

"Yeah, I know. He had some dreams about

living here and things being the way they used to be." James shook his head. "It would be nice, but things can't ever be what they used to be. A person can go home, but life and time changes us all."

"I think he knows it won't be the same. He just wants to come home."

"Right." James leaned back in his chair and he didn't look her way. "I should have put my foot down and we should have stayed here. But that's how life is. You make choices and you can't take them back."

"Very true."

"I'm sorry you lost him, Sophie." James patted her hand, finally smiling a bittersweet smile and looking at her. "I'm sorry things couldn't have been different for you."

"Life is what it is, James. I've had a good life. I've done what I wanted."

"You haven't married and had kids. Seems to me those would have been things you wanted."

"I haven't met anyone." She looked away, because his eyes had filled with tears. "I haven't stayed single because of Kade. I missed him for a long time. Sometimes I still do. But I haven't married because I haven't met anyone to marry."

"And you still have that rule about not dating bull riders." He laughed a little.

Sophie smiled at him. "Yes, I have that rule."

"Shame, because I think you and Keeton—"

She had to stop him there. "James, Keeton and I are friends."

"Yeah, I know." He drifted back to other thoughts, she could see it in his eyes, the way they clouded with other emotions. "I shouldn't have taught those boys to ride bulls. If I hadn't…"

She touched his arm and tried to find the right words. She thought about lectures she'd given herself over the years, and words of wisdom shared with her by her parents. She didn't have her own advice for him, but she had recycled advice that had worked for her.

"We can't always second-guess the decisions we made, or blame ourselves for the way life happens. We have to trust that God has a plan and that whatever happens, if we stand on faith, He'll get us through."

"That ride changed everything."

"One moment usually does have a way of changing everything. That's how life works."

"But you and Kade would have been married. We'd still be here on this land, married and with grandkids."

"We don't know that for sure." She touched his arm and he smiled at her. "Kade and I might not have gotten married. We were young. There are things we learn as we get older. One of those things is that sometimes what we think is love is really puppy love. But when we're young, we don't want to believe that."

"Yeah, I guess that's the truth." He nodded toward the end of the drive. "Here comes Keeton."

Keeton parked and had barely gotten out of his truck when Jackson pulled up the drive, going a little too fast. Sophie stood, her heart sinking a little. Keeton was taking Lucy from her car seat and he turned to look at her as she walked across the lawn to her brother.

"Soph, we just got a call for first responders at your building site. Gabe saw smoke and called the fire department."

"No." Her breath left her and she shook her head. Moments that change everything. "Why is this happening?"

Jackson shook his head. "I don't have a clue. But one way or the other, we'll figure it out and stop them. If you want, I'll drive you down there."

She looked at Keeton, who had left the sleeping baby in her car seat and moved forward. Why?

"Go. I'm going to help Dad get back upstairs. I'll meet you in a few." He touched her back, and then he moved away.

Sophie followed Jackson to his truck. She could drive herself but his truck was still running and it would be easier, better to have fewer cars taking up space when the fire trucks were trying to get to the house.

They were at the building site in less than two minutes. Sophie jumped out of the truck as it rolled to a stop. The fire truck was there. She watched Jackson hurry toward the truck where Travis and others were already in their protective gear. She watched from a distance as her brothers and the other volunteers from the Dawson Rural Fire Department went to work. Not that they could save the Tillers' house.

She knew that their intentions were to keep the fire from spreading to the house frame that had been started a week ago.

Keeton rolled up the drive in his truck. He had his dad and Lucy with him. Sophie stood her ground but her feet weren't planted as solidly as she'd once thought. Her feet wanted to walk her in the direction of Keeton. She remained steady, flicking her gaze from Keeton, Lucy and James on his crutches, back to the fire. A minute later Keeton stood next to her.

"I'm sorry." His voice, husky and soft, resonated deep inside her.

"It's okay. I mean, we'll start over."

"Yeah, of course." He had Lucy in one arm and he slid the other around her waist and pulled her to his side in a quick hug. Too quick.

"Why is this happening?" She looked up at him, into dark eyes. He shook his head.

"I don't have a clue, Sophie. I wish I did. I'd go after them myself if I knew who did this."

A truck pulled up the drive. A few of her workers. Jason, Gabe, Tucker. They got out of the truck and hurried toward her. Jason's face turned red and he shoved clenched fists deep in his pockets.

"What is going on with this town?" Jason looked from Keeton to her.

"I wish I knew." Sophie held her arms out and took Lucy, because it made it easier to bear, holding the baby girl who just loved and wanted to be loved.

Her heart melted a little more each time she held a baby that wasn't hers. Lucy cooed and smiled. In that smile Sophie saw Keeton, his smile, his eyes.

"Sweet baby." She kissed Lucy's cheek. And then she saw another truck, familiar, and one she hadn't wanted to see pulling up at that moment.

"Uh-oh." Keeton took Lucy from her. "Looks like your dad caught on."

Sophie nodded and walked away from the group of men. She stood next to her dad's truck when he got out. He didn't smile. He looked past her, at the fire. Then he looked at her. She was a grown woman. He had gray hair now. And she was still his kid.

"Why did you keep this a secret? We could have been helping you."

Sophie smiled and linked her arm through his. "That's why I kept it a secret, Dad."

"Because you don't want our help?"

They started walking, but not fast. "Dad, I needed to do something on my own. This is my project. I came up with the idea. I developed the plan. I got the funding and put it all together."

"On your own." He grinned and shook his head. "I'm proud of you. A little worried, but proud. How'd you come up with this land?"

"Clarence and Mary Gordon had to sell out after he got hurt. They sold their old home but then they couldn't sell this. They had remortgaged to pay bills, then couldn't make payments. I happened to be in town the day that it sold on the courthouse steps."

"I didn't realize things had gotten that bad for them."

"I didn't want to buy it out from under them." Sophie stared at the remaining embers that were once a house frame. "I called them before I bought it and they were done. They were tired of fighting to keep everything. After I bought this land I offered to let them have part of it back."

"They didn't want it?"

"No. They said they had already decided to move to town when their house sold. I put them in as managers of Golden Oaks." Golden Oaks was one of several apartment complexes owned by Cooper Holdings.

"I wondered about that." Her dad hugged her. "You make me proud. And I see their nephew is even here helping with the houses."

"Gabe. Yes. He needed something to do while he draws unemployment. Dad, you understand, don't you. Why I had to do this on my own?"

In a family with twelve kids, and revolving extras, having something of her own meant having her own identity. Her dad nodded, because of course he got it. He had to get it.

"I understand. But you can have help and still maintain control."

"Right." She laughed at his statement. "It always works out that way in this family. There's Jackson, fighting the fire. Lucky will be here in ten minutes. You're here."

"Is it that bad, having a family that is always here for you?"

"Not bad. Just sometimes a person needs their own thing and a little space."

He sighed and nodded. "I know. I get that. But you have to cut me a little slack. It's hard to be a dad and to know that all of your kids are grown and can walk without holding your hand."

"I still need you to hold my hand."

"Good thing, because I hadn't planned on letting go." He laughed, out of the blue, unexpectedly. "Why did I see Lucky's mule in your corral?"

Oops. She bit down on her bottom lip and tried to look innocent, clueless. It didn't work. Her dad knew how to read his kids. She'd never been the one playing the cute and innocent card.

"I'm not sure?" She smiled a little and they both laughed. "Okay, the truth is, Lucky's mule doesn't like Lucky. But he loves me. He's in the corral because I saddled him up this morning. And because he hangs out in there, hoping for grain."

"You've got to be kidding. How long has this been going on?"

"Since a week after the mule got loose. I kind of have a plan and I hope you won't tell."

"What's the plan?" One thing she could count on with her dad—he was always up for a good prank.

"I'm going to ride him in the opening parade of the rodeo this month."

"Until then you're going to let Lucky think his mule can't be caught."

"That's my plan."

"I won't tell." He kissed the top of her head. "I

never would have thought you'd be my girl out here building houses and breaking mules."

"Well, with Mia away, someone had to keep this family guessing."

"I miss her."

Sophie smiled at that. Mia had given their parents a hard time as a teenager. And they missed her. She had to admit, they weren't the only ones. "Yeah, me, too."

Keeton walked up to them, cowboy cute in faded jeans and a short-sleeved button-up shirt. He tipped his hat and nodded at her dad before looking at her. "They found a hot spot at the back of the house. Looks as if someone used gasoline. They didn't leave the cans this time."

"It still doesn't make sense. Your house and now this. What are they trying to do?" Sophie hadn't thought of giving up, not once. But today going forward wasn't as easy, not with the entire frame of the Tillers' house gone. But people were counting on her. She couldn't walk away from this project. It meant too much to too many people.

But she really could use a break.

Keeton found it a lot easier to look at the charred remains of the house rather than at Sophie. She wouldn't give up, but she looked like a person who might be having serious doubts.

"It could be the two places aren't connected." Keeton had been thinking that since they rolled up the drive and saw the house on fire.

"Then what other explanation would there be?" Sophie walked arm in arm with her dad. They got close to the burned house and could feel the heat from the still-smoldering fire.

"We'll just have to keep digging." Keeton pulled a handkerchief from his pocket and mopped his brow. "This is a real shame."

"Yeah, it is." Sophie walked a little closer and her dad reached for her arm, holding her back. "I won't get too close."

"I need to get Lucy home." He held the fussy little girl in his arms. Sophie had given her back to him when her dad showed up. It seemed to him the more Sophie was around, the more his baby girl wanted Sophie and not him.

Sophie nodded but her gaze had drifted to the burned house, her expression shadowed with sorrow and anger. "I have to stay and talk to the police."

"Let me take you out later."

She opened her mouth, closed it and smiled. "You almost caught me at a weak moment."

He laughed. "No bull riders."

"No."

"That's a dating rule. Did you ever stop to think a bull rider could make a very good friend?"

Tim Cooper said something neither of them caught and he walked away. Keeton watched Sophie's dad put his arm around Jackson, then the two talked and then walked around the charred remains of the house. Keeton focused on the woman standing in front of him, her head turned so that he caught her profile, the sad smile.

"Keeton, you scare me." She shrugged one shoulder. "We keep doing this dance, pretending we're friends, pretending nothing has ever happened, and we both know it's a lie."

"Then stop pretending and let's maybe reconsider a few of your rules. Or break a few."

"I can't lose you."

"You won't." He reached for her hand and she looked up, meeting his eyes.

"I lost you once before. I lost your friendship. I didn't see you for years."

"You're not going to lose me." He took a step that put him next to her, he looked over her shoulder at the crowd of people, some watching them, some not. Her dad turned and then looked away.

"I'm not going to take that chance."

"So even friendship is off-limits?"

She pulled her hand free. "Of course we're friends."

Good, that gave him something to work with.

Whether she wanted to admit it or not, she'd left a door open.

"I'll see you at your place." He turned, just feet away from her. "Do you want me to feed that mule, and then chase him out of your corral before Lucky drives past and sees him?"

"That would be good." Her smile beamed, chasing shadows from her eyes.

He nodded once. "See you at home."

See you at home. The words bounced between them. Yeah, he'd like for that to be something he could say for the rest of his life. While he had those thoughts, Sophie looked as if she had a bunch of regret piling up.

He winked as he walked away, hoping to keep the mood light. Sophie walked to where her dad stood. He saw them talking as he got his dad and Lucy in the truck. Sophie nodded when he waved.

An hour later he had settled Lucy in her baby swing, his dad was watching her. He'd gone down to the corral to let the mule loose. He watched as the big, red animal walked calmly out of the gate, took a few running steps and jumped the fence to trot off down the road.

Amazing. No wonder mules were so popular with hunters. He'd always been a quarterhorse guy himself, but he might consider getting a mule after being around Sophie's. Make that

Lucky's. As he watched the animal trot down the road, Jackson's truck pulled in the drive and Sophie got out.

He started to walk down to greet her, but on second thought he stood his ground, willing to let her make the next move. She talked to her brother for a second through the open truck window and then she turned to walk up the path to her back door. She looked tired. She actually looked beat. At the porch of the big, stone house she stopped for a minute. She looked up at the steps, as if they were more than she could handle. He waited. She didn't seem to notice him.

Something about her slow steps worried him. It would be easy, to go back to his little apartment, to his dad and his daughter, but something stopped him. That same something acted as a force to push him to her house, to knock on the front door.

She didn't answer. He knocked again. After a few minutes she appeared, pale, shaking.

He opened the door and she backed away.

"I'm sick." She turned and ran down the hall. At the bathroom door she stopped and turned. "You should go so you don't catch it."

"I'm not going anywhere. I'd say you caught it from Lucy. If I was going to catch it, I'm guessing I'd already have it." He walked into the bathroom with her, the last place he probably really wanted to be.

She had sat on the floor and she leaned against the cabinets, her knees pulled up, her head resting on them. He thought about being a hero and picking her up and he laughed at the image that came to mind.

"Is this funny?" She looked up, pale, unsmiling. Her mascara had smeared. He reached for a washcloth and kneeled to wipe her face.

"No, this isn't." He wiped the smudges of mascara, not an easy task. "I considered being a hero and picking you up. In my mind it made sense, to carry you to the living room."

"You couldn't pick me up, you're old."

"I'm not old."

"You have a bad knee and I'm not some petite woman a man sweeps off her feet." She moved fast. "Leave, I'm going to be sick again and I really don't think you standing here is romantic."

"Gotcha." He was starting to feel a little queasy himself.

He wandered to the kitchen and found tea. Hot tea would have to be good. And crackers. He had a cup of water in the microwave and crackers on a plate when she walked in, looking a little shaky on her feet.

"Sit down."

She nodded and complied, sitting at the little

table in the center of the kitchen. He guessed that table got a lot more use than the massive oak table in the formal dining room. When he finished the tea and took it to her, her head rested on her arms and her hair covered her face.

"You sleeping?" He set the cup and plate in front of her and took the seat next to hers.

She looked up, eyes watery and face flushed. "No, just trying to make things stop spinning. Didn't I tell you just a few hours ago that we aren't going to work?"

"You said we could be friends. And friends take care of each other."

She reached for the cup of tea. "Thank you."

"You're welcome. And I'm even going to forgive that statement about me being old."

She smiled over the rim of the cup and took a sip. When she put the cup back on the saucer he touched her cheek.

"You're hot." He guessed she probably knew that.

"Yeah."

"You should go lie down."

"I don't want to. It's early. I have things to do."

"I let the mule out for you. Go lie down. I'll run over and get Lucy and be right back."

"Keeton, you don't have to. I'm a grown woman. I've been taking care of myself for a long time."

"I know I don't have to. I want to." He didn't tell her that he couldn't leave her alone. The idea of him sitting in her guesthouse while she was here alone didn't sit well. Not just because she was sick, but because someone seemed pretty serious about burning down houses.

"I'm going to stretch out on the couch and watch TV." She stood, wobbling a little.

Keeton slid an arm around her waist and she didn't protest, instead she leaned into him. They sighed at the same time. Resignation?

Sophie settled on the sofa and he pulled an afghan off the back of a nearby rocking chair and pulled it over her. She reached for the remote and smiled up at him, a sleepy smile. "Go take care of Lucy and your dad."

"You're very bossy and I don't boss well." He leaned to kiss the top of her head.

As he walked across the yard a few minutes later he had a real moment of wondering when and how this had become his life. A month ago he'd been living his own life, making decisions for himself. Today he had a daughter, his dad and now Sophie. Connections that kept a guy grounded.

He hadn't expected all of this when he came home to Dawson. He'd had plans that included his land, maybe helping his dad get his life back. Sophie might have been there, lingering in the back of his mind, but he hadn't allowed her to be his reason for coming back.

Now he realized she was very much a part of his return.

Chapter Ten

Soft lamplight glowed, casting shadows on the living-room wall. Sophie rolled to her side and jumped a little, her heart responding to the man across from her by kicking into fast forward. She hadn't expected him to be there when she woke up. But he was. Keeton sat in her big chair with Lucy curled in one arm and a book in his other hand.

She watched him for a long minute, stretched out in her chair, his soft, white button-up shirt, faded jeans, and his dark hair a little messy from running his hand through it, or from his hat. He looked up, smiling when he saw that she watched him.

"How are you?" He put the book down on the table next to the chair. She smiled because he must not have found the bookcase. He'd picked up a romance novel she'd been reading.

"Good. Are you enjoying the book?"

He grinned and raised a shoulder in a slight shrug. "I'm learning a lot. There are lines I didn't know a guy should use. And things I should notice that I haven't."

"Like what?" She scooted up to a sitting position, pulling the afghan around her shoulders. A glass of water had been placed on the table next to her. She reached for it.

"Sophie, when I look into your eyes, I see forever."

"Really, because I think you see scorn."

He laughed and reached for the book again. "Maybe I said that wrong."

"Maybe you should stop while you're ahead."

He put the book back on the table. "I probably should. But it doesn't hurt a guy to learn what women want to hear. I'd say if it's in a romance novel, then that's what women expect."

"It's fiction. Real men smell bad when they sweat, say the wrong things and aren't there." She stopped at the unfairness of the last statement. "No, real men are there when you need them. Thank you for staying with me."

"My pleasure, ma'am." His grin so cute she wanted to forget reservations, that part of her brain that triggered when he was around, telling her to hold back, don't get attached.

"Maybe you should take that book home with

you." She leaned against the arm of the couch. "I feel very bad for Lucy. I had no idea how cruddy she felt."

"I'm sorry you got sick."

"I'll be fine. It isn't your fault." She started to get up, but he was on his feet ahead of her.

"What do you need?"

She held back laughter. She hadn't been taken care of like this since she left home years ago. And he was the last person she'd expected to play nursemaid, the cowboy in his scuffed boots and well-worn jeans. But then, he'd been surprising her a lot lately.

"I wanted to get some aspirin. And maybe a sandwich."

"You know there's no food in this house other than peanut butter." He leaned over the playpen and laid Lucy down. The baby rolled to her side and kept sleeping.

"I happen to like peanut butter." She thought again. "Maybe not tonight."

"I brought a can of chicken soup from my place. If I heat it up will you eat it?"

"I would." She sighed. She couldn't keep doing this. "Keeton, you don't owe me. You don't have to take care of me like I'm one of your responsibilities."

He turned but didn't walk back to her. The lamplight cast him in a warm glow of light, his face in shadows. He didn't smile as he stared at her.

"What do you think, Sophie, that I'm here out of guilt, because of something that happened years ago that neither of us could have stopped?"

"I don't know." She brushed a hand across her face and tried to make thoughts stop swirling through her brain. "I don't know. There's a part of me that thinks there's an 'us.' And then I think that we are just products of what happened and that you're here in my life out of a sense of duty to Kade. And I don't want to always question that."

He stood in the center of her living room, his hands behind his back, his head down. He let out a long sigh and shook his head. "I'm going to be real honest with you, Sophie. There are times that I question myself and wonder if that's why I'm here. But I've never thought you needed to be taken care of. If that was the real reason for my being here, wouldn't I have been here all along?"

"Have you forgiven yourself?" Because years ago he'd told her he would never forgive himself. And never is a long time.

He looked up at the ceiling, and then he nodded. "Yeah, I have. It ate at me for a few very long years. Eventually I realized I had to stop blaming myself, blaming God, blaming the stupid bull. Kade was doing what he loved to do."

"I know he was."

Dark eyes held hers. "Have you forgiven me for pulling that bull rope?"

She had hit him. Over and over again when they'd told her Kade was gone, she'd hit Keeton. As if he could have stopped it from happening. "I don't blame you."

"Have you forgiven me?"

She nodded. "I forgave you a long, long time ago."

They both knew what was between them. They knew their past. They knew what separated them. And now she knew he wasn't here out of guilt. So where did that leave them?

It left them here, with Keeton still chasing a dream that had never been his. Sophie had gotten used to life by herself and gotten used to not taking chances with her heart.

Guilt was between them, though. Because they'd turned to each other after Kade's funeral. And for years she'd told herself that what she'd felt in his arms had been comfort. They'd comforted each other. Nothing more.

She looked up at him as he turned to walk away. If she accepted what she felt as more than comfort, where did that leave them? With her still not wanting to take chances, and still afraid of the sport he wouldn't give up? She couldn't take that chance.

While he was in the kitchen she reached for her laptop. She needed to think about something other than Keeton, the fires were a good distraction. Who felt this strongly about a housing development, so strongly they'd burn homes? She sighed and leaned back on the couch because her head pounded and her stomach still rolled.

"What are you looking for?" Keeton handed her a tray with a bowl of soup and slices of apples. He'd definitely been reading her romance novel for a while. She smiled up at him.

"I really don't know. I just can't stop thinking about the land and who would want to burn down those homes."

"Maybe it isn't about the land." He pulled the ottoman from the chair close to the sofa and sat down. "Maybe this is just about arson. Maybe someone is getting kicks by setting fires."

She hadn't really thought about that. "Okay, maybe."

She picked up the spoon and he took the computer from her lap. He didn't go back to his seat. He lowered himself to the edge of the couch and sat next to her. "Think about it. My house isn't attached to what you're doing."

"So it has to be about who wants the land?"

"I'm not selling. Are you?" He typed in some information on the search engine.

"No, I'm not going to be run off this way."

Keeton closed the computer and set it on the table. "I don't think there's an easy answer. But I want you to be careful."

Sophie did not want to kiss him. She did not. She told herself a couple of times, in case she didn't get it the first time. But he was sweet, and no longer a boy looking for himself, for who he wanted to be. She wasn't a girl, trying to find a way to heal the hole inside her heart.

All of that added up made her more afraid than she'd been all of those years ago. Because what was there to stop them, to come between them? And she didn't want another broken heart. *Broken* probably hadn't been the right word. *Shattered* was more like it. The years that most girls her age had spent dating and falling in love, she'd spent getting over a broken heart.

That had been a long time ago. Now she was definitely not a girl. Her heart had long since healed. And Keeton West did things to her insides that she couldn't begin to fathom. The air between them felt like electricity, like summer air before a storm hit.

Fear and courage were duking it out inside her. She was on one hand afraid to take a chance, and on the other wanting nothing more than a chance to be loved by someone like him.

He touched her chin and his fingers slid to her neck.

"I'm sick." She backed away.

Keeton nodded and stood up. "I should go."

"You should."

"Will you call if you need anything?"

"I'll be fine. I'm a big girl, Keeton." She smiled to prove it. He brushed fingers through her hair. She shivered at the gentle touch.

"I'm going."

He gathered Lucy up from the playpen and reached for the diaper bag. At the arched door that led to the entryway of her house he stopped. "I'm sure you're used to taking care of yourself. But, Soph, we don't know who these people are or what they're after. If you hear or see anything that worries you, call my cell."

"I will." She didn't walk him to the door. Her legs were weak, shaking. And not because she was sick.

After he'd left she told herself this wasn't real. She was sick. She was emotional. Keeton was sweet and easy to look at. Tomorrow, when she felt better, she'd get things in perspective.

She reminded herself that she'd already told him she wouldn't date a bull rider. It was easy-peasy if she remembered that rule.

But when he treated her this way, as though

she mattered, it made it harder to remember why she'd ever stopped dating bull riders. And it also made her think that there should be exceptions to every rule.

Keeton's mom showed up two days after the fire. He had just met with Jeremy Hightree concerning the business they'd opened the previous fall. So far the motorcycle dealership had rocked and it kept rocking. But did that make it easier to see his mom sitting on Sophie's front porch, Sophie in the chair next to her? Not really. He was suddenly the one being rocked.

At least Sophie seemed to be better. He'd worried about leaving her for an entire day. Yeah, he knew the Coopers had been supplying her with food, stopping to check on her, and Heather had even spent one night. But he'd worried about her when he drove off this morning.

He parked his truck under the carport next to her car. After unbuckling Lucy from the car seat he lifted his daughter and walked up the sidewalk to Sophie's.

His dad hobbled across the yard on crutches.

Dread or hope? Keeton didn't know which to feel. Maybe both suited the situation. What in the world had he thought, coming back here? Yeah, that was a good question.

He stopped on the bottom step, Lucy in the

crook of his arm. He turned her so his mom could see her granddaughter for the first time.

"Lucy, meet Grandma. Mom, this is your granddaughter, Lucy." He walked up the steps to the front porch, shaded by the arched, stone columns.

"She's beautiful, Keeton." His mom held out her arms and he handed over his daughter. It was still new to him, that Lucy was his.

He hadn't seen her birth. He hadn't watched her grow inside her mom, or gone to prenatal doctor's visits. He hadn't had time to prepare for this. But it suited him, he decided. Yeah, he liked being a dad. He liked everything about it.

As his mom rocked Lucy, his dad came up the steps. He eased down on to the wicker love-seat across from the women. Keeton smiled at Sophie. She looked better than she had the first night, but still pale. Of course she hadn't been to the doctor. She said it was a virus, she didn't need to go.

"How are you?" He sat down next to his dad and smiled at Sophie.

"Good. How about you?"

He grinned at that and looked from his mom to his dad. Sophie smiled, too.

"Good."

His parents in Dawson at the same time. He hadn't really thought about that happening. One thing he'd learned in his life was to trust God's plan. Trust that sometimes God used people's plans to carry out His greater plan.

Or maybe it was more wishful thinking, that his parents would find a way to work things out. All these years later and he was still the kid thinking his mom and dad might get back together. He shook his head at that. He definitely didn't qualify as a kid.

He'd gone to the doctor for his knee and was looking at knee replacement in the next ten years. Yeah, way past being a kid. He'd also been told he should think about quitting. No, he didn't get "doctor's orders" to stop riding bulls, just a strong recommendation.

Stop riding bulls. He refocused on Lucy, who had hold of her grandmother's shoulder-length hair. If he quit, what would he do? He had options. He could get a job teaching. He could start a bull-riding school. Or he could keep working with Jeremy.

"What's up?" Sophie leaned close to ask the question.

He smiled at her and shrugged. "Nothing, just a lot to think about."

"Everything okay?"

"Yeah, everything's okay." He touched her hand but stopped short of lacing his fingers through hers, the way he wanted to. "How are you feeling?"

"Good. No fever today."

"Glad to hear that. Is there anything I can do for you? The grass is getting pretty high. I can mow."

She leaned, touching her shoulder against his. "No, I have a guy who does that. He's on a limited income and…"

"Yeah, I get it. But let me know."

"Have you seen the mule in the last couple of days?" She switched topics, taking him by surprise.

"Yeah, he was at the pond today. What are you going to do about that mule? Eventually Lucky is going to see him."

"I kind of thought I'd see if you would trailer him to the rodeo in a couple of weeks. I'm going to ride him in the opening parade." She smiled and lifted her brows. He laughed.

"That would require riding him. Right?"

She held a finger to her lips and he turned, smiling at his suddenly silent parents. Sophie saved the day. "So, Doris, how long are you staying?"

"Just for the night. I'm staying with a friend and I have to be back at work tomorrow." His mom leaned to kiss Lucy. "But I have to admit it will be hard to leave this little sweetheart."

"You can stay here," Sophie offered. "I have plenty of room. That will give you more time with Lucy and Keeton."

His mom smiled at Sophie. "That's really sweet, but I don't want to take advantage. I think you have plenty of my family members staying here."

"They aren't taking advantage and you won't be, either. If you want to stay, you're more than welcome." Sophie stood, and Keeton had a moment where he wondered how he had ever let her go. All of those years ago, why hadn't he fought to keep her in his life?

Because he'd decided back then that in his arms, she'd always be thinking about his brother. He had worried that she'd compare them and he'd come out on the short end of the stick.

But a woman like Sophie shouldn't be ignored, let go of or taken for granted. She was beautiful, classy and down-to-earth. All in one pretty, amazing package.

She had opened the door to go in and she paused. "Would you all like coffee?"

His parents nodded, but their attention was focused on Lucy and he wasn't sure if they actually heard.

Keeton followed her through the front door. "Hey, wait up."

She turned, smiling at him. "What's wrong?"

"Nothing, I thought I could help since Lucy is busy entertaining her grandparents."

"Right, okay."

He thought about turning and walking away. Instead he reached for her and pulled her close. He held her tight and she held him back. Man, she felt good in his arms, her hands on his back. The scent of her, the feel of her, it filled up empty spaces inside him and he thought maybe he'd hold her forever.

He would if he could.

After a minute of holding her he stepped back, breaking contact but first kissing right next to her ear. "I needed that."

She brushed her hands down his arms. "I knew I needed something, I didn't realize that's what it was. Thank you."

"You're welcome."

They walked to the kitchen together. "It's a big deal, having your parents in Dawson together." Sophie pulled the coffeepot out.

"Yeah, it is. I didn't think about it, about the two of them showing up at the same time like this. I'm a grown man, but I still would like to see them work things out."

She turned from pouring water in the coffee maker. "I don't think that's so unusual. Years ago when Mom found out about Jeremy being my dad's son, I thought my parents would divorce.

I guess I was considered an adult at the time, barely. But even at that age, I didn't want them to split up. I thought about all of us not together at holidays and how it would feel to have a wedding…"

Her voice trailed off.

"But they stuck it out. They'll both be there, for every big moment in your life."

"I've had big moments. They've been there. I'm not a kid, still dreaming about those things."

Those things? He watched her pour coffee in mugs. "You're breaking my heart, Soph. Are you telling me I'm too old for weddings and babies? Because I love the one I have and I've been thinking she'll need brothers and sisters. Maybe I need to stop reading that romance novel of yours."

"Just because I'm a happy spinster doesn't mean you have to stop dreaming." She handed him a cup. "And if I had a Lucy, I'd want a dozen more."

He could tell Sophie one better. He'd held her and he could imagine holding her for the rest of his life. Which meant he needed to get his parents and head for his place before he said too much.

Sophie watched Keeton and his family leave a short time later. His family. His parents. His daughter. She let out a sigh and closed the door so she could lean against it. And then slide down to the floor and sit.

She had to go do something. She had to get out of this house. She hadn't stayed inside for this many days in a row since…she couldn't remember.

A few minutes later she walked out the back door in linen capris and a light cotton blouse. It amazed her, that the simple of act of changing into something lighter, less like pajamas, could make her feel so much better.

As she drove down the road she made plans. Where to go? She decided on the Bible study at church. For some reason she hadn't been going lately. Not because she didn't enjoy it. She'd just gotten out of the habit. Or maybe she'd gotten tired of being the only single person in attendance. Everyone her age had a husband, wife, kids, and the stories or prayers requests that went with those things.

She didn't even have a cat or a dog. She had a mule that no one had known about until recently. She had a project she enjoyed keeping to herself, until that too became public knowledge.

And when she walked through the doors of the church, she realized other things were public knowledge. Lucky's wife, Anna, smirked and elbowed Jana Tiller. They both looked her way, nodded and then whispered.

Of course they headed straight for her.

Too late to leave, the door appeared to be blocked by people either sharing news or trying to hold her hostage. She steadied herself for the assault.

"So, how's it going?" Anna smiled big and hugged her. "Are you feeling better?"

"Much better." She dug her Bible out of her bag. "So good, in fact, I thought I'd join you all for Bible study. When do we start?"

"Fifteen minutes." Anna looped her arm through Sophie's. "You haven't been here in a while."

"I know. I started thinking about that and realized it's been months. Is there coffee?"

Third attempt to get conversation off herself and on to a more neutral topic. Another fail.

Anna led her toward the coffeepot, almost fooling her. "I heard that Keeton West stayed with you the other evening."

"Really?"

At that, Anna laughed. She had pretty blue eyes and a smile that lit up her face. Lucky had loved her since preschool. They'd married right after college. Anna had once apologized to Sophie, because Sophie should have married

Kade first. It should have been her walking down the aisle with her best friend.

Best friend. She faltered at the words and had to collect herself quick because Anna had handed her a cup of hot coffee. When she thought about best friends she thought about Keeton, about summers at the creek, riding horses on trail rides, sometimes arguing over silly stuff.

She coughed to cover her lapse. Anna stared, and then smiled.

"I think you're not really over that virus." Anna covered for her, smiling at a few of the other attendees who stood nearby.

"I'm good." She took a sip and gave herself a few seconds reprieve, thanks to her sister-in-law. "I'm all better."

Lucky appeared, carrying a notebook and his Bible. "Hey, sis, glad to see you here."

He hugged her tight.

"It's good to be here."

Stop with the easy conversation. She loved them all but light conversation and deep, questioning looks didn't match. She wasn't about to lose it. She wasn't going to fall apart because Keeton West had moved back to Dawson.

Not because of the past anyway.

Maybe it was the present that had really started to get to her.

Chapter Eleven

Two days after the Bible study that hadn't changed her life but had pulled her back into her old group, old friends, Sophie pulled up to the building site and climbed out of her truck. Now that everyone knew that this project, the land and the nonprofit were hers, she guessed she didn't really need to go incognito. But she kind of liked the old truck she'd bought a few months back. The seats were worn but comfortable. The radio played static with the occasional country music lyrics or talk radio filtering in.

Yeah, old trucks were special. She was a little disappointed that Keeton had shipped his off as soon as his new one got delivered the previous week. His had reminded her of riding to town with her grandfather, windows down and an ice cream cone melting down her arm as she tried like crazy to finish before they got home.

Gabe pounded a few nails into the frame of

the house he had been working on, shoved his hammer into his tool belt and walked down to greet her. He glanced around, looking a little unsure. Maybe because he'd been working alone again and she'd told him he really didn't have to spend every day here.

It was Saturday, he could go home and relax, hang out with friends, maybe grill hamburgers. When she told him that, he grinned and told her he'd rather be busy.

They walked up to the house together. "Do you think you should keep doing this, Ms. Cooper? I mean, it's starting to seem kind of dangerous. I'm not sure these houses are worth someone getting hurt over."

He wasn't a tall guy, but he looked tall because of his broad build. His shaggy brown hair, covered with a ball cap, tended to frizz in this hot weather. He didn't look like a guy that would be afraid.

"I'm not going to let someone scare me off, Gabe."

"No, ma'am, I didn't think you would." He grinned and reached for another two-by-four. "I'm just worried, that's all. Someone sure seems bent out of shape."

"Yes, well, I'm not sure if that's the case."

He looked up, brows arching under the bill of his hat. "What do you think it is then?"

"The police are looking more at kids vandalizing, and not realizing what a serious crime they're committing."

"I guess I don't agree. But you stay safe, you hear?"

"I'll stay safe."

The sound of cars, tires on pavement, all moving their way caught her attention. Sophie turned and watched as a dozen trucks in a row turned onto the gravel road that would someday be a paved street.

"What in the world?" Gabe straightened and watched the procession of vehicles.

"I don't have a clue."

At the front of the line she recognized Jackson's truck, Lucky's, Keeton's and then more that she didn't know. As they parked she walked toward them. Jackson got out of his truck, and then reached into the back to grab a toolbox.

"What are you doing?" she called out as she got closer.

Her brother grinned, big. "Someone called in the troops."

"What?"

He nodded in the direction of Keeton's truck. "Keeton arranged it. With all of the problems you've had getting this project off the ground, he thought it would be good if we all chipped in, donated some time and got these houses going."

"Who are all of these people?"

"Family, friends and the Jorgensons."

A local Mennonite family. "I can't believe this."

"Believe it. By the end of the day these two houses will be framed, and then some."

Sophie wiped at her eyes. "Jackson, this is wonderful."

"Don't cry, you'll make Lucky cry. Not me, just Lucky. You know how softhearted he is. And besides that, it's Keeton. He made the calls."

She turned and Keeton stood behind her. Lucy wasn't with him. Her heart nearly came apart at the seams. "Thank you."

It seemed simple, thank him and don't throw herself into his arms. But his crooked smile, dark eyes that lit up with laughter, yeah, it made it hard not to hug him tight.

But she had a reputation to uphold. She smoothed her hands down the sides of her jeans and managed a fairly mature, although slightly trembling, smile. She knew how to be cool, to be professional. She knew how to hold back and not let emotions get the better of her.

She knew how to keep things to herself. Or at least once upon a time that had been the case.

"You look like you're recovered," he finally said.

"I'm good. I can't believe you did this."

"I've been gone a long time, Sophie, but I know how things are done in Dawson. People look out for each other. This is your town looking out for you."

"I'm amazed." More than amazed. She watched as the men who had arrived to help started hauling tools out of their trucks, pulling on work gloves and getting ready to start on this job. Last night she'd been a little hopeless over this situation. And now? God was obviously reminding her who she should have hope in.

She'd had a great idea, people said. But God had brought it all about. She needed to remember that. This happened to be a very good reminder of that fact. With the frame of one house gone, there had been serious questions about finding the money to start over.

"Where's Lucy?"

"With my mom."

He turned as men gathered, waiting for the plan. And he had one. He laid it all out on the paper he'd brought. The men split into groups and went to work.

Sophie turned to look for Gabe. He'd left. She shook her head, wondering why. Maybe he really did like to work alone. Or maybe he wanted to take credit for the rebuilding and didn't want to share the glory? She hoped that wasn't the case.

"Is everything okay with Gabe?" Jackson approached, pulling on work gloves.

She smiled because Jackson had changed so much in the last six months or so. He had his wife, Madeline, his daughter, Jade, and now they were planning to adopt. One woman had brought him to this new place, where he fit the role of husband, father and automatic caretaker.

Everyone was getting married, having families, settling down. She thought about some of the men who had asked her out, and she'd turned them down because she'd been busy or not interested. The few she'd gone out with, she'd dated only once or twice. She didn't see a reason to invest time in relationships that were going nowhere.

"Sophie?" Jackson poked her and she jumped a little. "Gabe?"

"What do you mean?"

"He walked down through the woods, and then he came back up, got in his truck and left."

"I don't know. I wonder if maybe he wanted to be able to say he saved the day but then you guys all showed up?"

"Could be." Jackson glanced toward the road. Gabe was long gone. "That's probably it. I'd like it if you didn't come over here alone for a while."

"I wasn't alone. Gabe was here."

Jackson gave her a pointed look. "That's what I mean."

"I'm not afraid and I don't need for you guys to start worrying and taking over. I appreciate the help. I'm all for the help. But I'm careful. I'm not going to take chances. Trust me on that."

"What guys?" He smiled and laughed a little, as if he didn't hear anything but that. "Oh, is Keeton giving you the same warning?"

"He is. And this is why I don't share my business with everyone. And since you tried to keep Jade from us in the beginning, you should be more understanding."

"Point taken. But don't forget you have a family. And admit it, all of this help is probably going to save a lot of money."

She closed her eyes briefly and then opened them and smiled at her brother. "I'm blessed beyond belief."

"By a tribe of people who get in your business. Don't worry, I get it. I really do."

He got it because it hadn't worked any better for him than it was for Sophie. Being a Cooper meant having a dozen siblings and two very loving parents involved in your life. Oh, and Grandma Myrna.

"I know you get it." She hugged him. "And I'm glad you're here to help."

"I didn't say I'm here to do everything." He

handed her a hammer. "If you're getting your name on this project, I'd say you'd best start hammering some nails."

"I can do that." She was a Cooper, after all.

As she went to work, she glanced back and saw Keeton watching her. He tipped his hat and then turned back to the work he was doing. She let herself enjoy a guilty little pleasure while no one paid attention. She watched Keeton work.

After a long day building houses, Keeton wasn't sure he would make it to the rodeo that night. He walked out of the guesthouse, cleaned up and ready to go. But his heart wasn't in it. Lucy squirmed in his arms, tugged at his collar and babbled.

Nothing in his life had made him want to settle down the way his little girl did. Of course that thought made him glance toward Sophie's house. He pulled keys out of his pocket and headed toward his truck. When he got home earlier he'd packed his gear. He'd wrapped his knee.

He hesitated midway to his truck, wondering what Sophie was doing. He hadn't seen her since he got home, but both her car and the old beater farm truck were here. His dad hadn't seen her, either.

Keeton's mom had decided to spend the weekend with Myrna Cooper, Sophie's grandmother.

He kind of thought that was her way of staying here, close to her granddaughter and to the ex-husband that needed a little extra help.

Sober wasn't an easy place for his dad. The last few days had been pretty rough on James West. They'd had some long nights, some long talks. Keeton had woken up that morning feeling as though he hadn't slept at all.

A loud noise and then a shout interrupted his thoughts and rattled his sleep-deprived brain. It came from behind Sophie's house. Keeton held Lucy tight and ran. He rounded the corner of the house and headed for the barn. Halfway across the yard he saw Sophie in the corral.

Sitting on that stupid mule.

The mule wasn't moving. Sophie used the reins to give it a whack, but the mule just wasn't going for this riding business. Sophie leaned and the big ears of the mule twitched. Keeton laughed, wondering if she was threatening the animal's life, or promising something sweet.

He'd been on the receiving end of her whispers. He preferred sweet promises.

Since it didn't seem to be a life-or-death situation he slowed and walked the rest of the way to the corral. Yeah, he wouldn't be going to the rodeo tonight. Instead he leaned against the fence, holding Lucy and watching what might be a better rodeo.

"I wouldn't make him mad," he warned.

Sophie shot him a look, nose wrinkling and mouth turning in a pretty frown. She'd pulled her hair back in a ponytail. "I think I know what I'm doing."

"I know you do. I'm just saying."

"Please don't." She used her heels on the mule's sides. The animal took two stiff-legged steps.

"Watch it."

"I'm watching. Stop distracting me."

"I'm just…"

Before he could finish the mule went straight up, and then bucked a few times. She held tight. The mule ran across the corral, bucking a few more times. Sophie's legs wrapped around the animal's belly and her head rocked back and then forward.

"Sophie!"

"Be quiet."

Right. Because she knew what she was doing. He held tight to Lucy and leaned over the fence, knowing he couldn't do a stinking thing but watch and hope she didn't land on the ground.

Cooper women were just as messed up as Cooper men when it came to stubborn. He sighed with relief when the mule settled into a walk with Sophie still on his back. She grinned and saluted him.

"Okay, you win." He eased out his breath and the words weren't easy.

"I know." She kept the mule in a halting walk around the arena. "This isn't the first time I've been on him."

"Well, you can get off now." Before he had a heart attack.

"No, I can't."

"Why?"

"I don't want him to think he won."

"Sophie, you're still on his back."

"I know that." Her back to him, she kept talking. "But if I get off now, he'll remember that he bucked and I got off."

Never argue with a woman. He said a silent prayer that she wouldn't break her neck and he watched as she continued to ride the big chestnut mule. Finally she pulled him to a stop and slid to the ground.

Never would he mention that he saw her legs tremble just a little. Of course, his legs would have trembled had he taken that ride. She turned, smiling, and led the mule to the fence.

"See." She tilted her head just a little.

"Yeah, I see. You won."

"Yep. And won't Lucky be surprised next week."

"At the Dawson Rodeo?"

"Yep." She rubbed her hand down the mule's neck. "He's nice, don't you think?"

"Uh, sure, if you like long ears and a stubborn personality." He'd have to rethink stubborn personalities. He thought he kind of liked people that were stubborn.

Stubborn enough to keep building houses, even when someone really wanted to stop her. Stubborn enough to stay on a mule, even when it wanted to toss her to the ground. Stubborn enough to keep telling him she wasn't interested.

Yeah, that part he needed to work on. The part where she didn't seem to be interested in him.

"I thought you were going to ride tonight?" she asked as she tied the mule and threw the stirrups over its back to unbuckle the cinch. She looked back over her shoulder at Keeton.

"I was going to but..." He looked down at Lucy and Sophie smiled.

"Yeah, some things are just better, aren't they?"

"Yeah, some things are." He shifted and moved Lucy to his other arm. Amazing how heavy she could get. "I'll go next week. I have to ride in Dawson. I have to be there to see the look on Lucky's face."

"Right." She pulled off the saddle, and then settled it on the top board of the corral fence. The mule turned to rub his head against her. She pushed his big head back, unbuckled the jaw strap and pulled off the bridle. "There you go, Lucky."

Keeton laughed, "I love it that you named him after your brother."

"It has a certain ring to it, doesn't it?"

"Yeah, it does."

A car turned and pulled up her drive. Sophie groaned. "This isn't going to be good."

Her grandmother got out of the car, dressed for church.

"Why's she all dressed up?" Keeton asked.

"Someone is in for a lecture. Those are her 'intervention' clothes. That means either me—" she looked at him "—or possibly you, is in for Granny Myrna's special kind of advice."

"Great."

"That means she's going to turn our lives around, and we'll think it was our idea."

"I should go." Keeton stepped away from the fence.

"Too late."

Granny Myrna waved a bejeweled hand and headed their way.

As she got closer she put on a big smile. Keeton loved Myrna Cooper. She had a big heart and a lot of love. And she meddled like nobody's business. But she knew how to do it without it really feeling like meddling. He groaned and Sophie giggled.

He turned, giving Sophie a look.

Before he could say anything, Myrna was upon them.

"Hi, Granny." Sophie walked through the gate after a last look back at the mule who stood at the opposite side of the corral waiting to be set free.

"Is that Lucky's mule?" Myrna walked up the fence. "It is Lucky's mule, and that's a saddle imprint on his back. Have you been riding that mule?"

Sophie nodded and her lips twitched in a smile. "I cannot tell a lie, Gran, I've been riding Lucky's mule."

Suddenly they were sixteen-year-old kids again. Keeton watched in wonder as the grown woman, a business professional, blushed and admitted to everything. He needed to get out of here fast, because there were things he didn't want to confess, not here, not in front of Sophie.

But Myrna had turned those eagle eyes on him. She pursed her lips and looked him over, head to toe. "Well, you'll do."

"Pardon?" He didn't have a clue, but he looked at Sophie and he kind of did.

"I said, you'll do." She stepped close. "You're strong. You know what you want out of life. You're a good man with Christian values. Yes, you'll do."

"I'm sorry, Mrs. Cooper, I'm not sure I know what you mean."

Myrna Cooper laughed. "Don't look so cornered, or so surprised. It isn't every day that a man comes along that I deem good enough for one of my granddaughters."

Sophie choked. She coughed. "Gran, Keeton and I, we're not…"

Keeton looked at her, struck by how beautiful she was, even with her hair pulled back in a messy ponytail, and a smudge of dirt across her cheek. He was sorry she wouldn't give them a chance.

"I know you're not." Myrna licked her finger and then rubbed the dirt off her granddaughter's face. "How could you catch a man looking the way you look? Go clean up and let him take you out to dinner."

"Myrna, we're just…"

Keeton didn't have any better luck. Myrna had hold of Sophie's hand and his. "I'm an old lady and I don't have much to keep me busy. I pray. I meddle. And I'm a mean matchmaker. Look how happy Jackson and Madeline are. Now, I'm going to let the two of you think about what I've said, but I expect great-grandchildren."

She touched Lucy's face. "And this one is good start."

"But, Granny." Sophie tried again.

"Don't 'Granny' me. I've been praying for you both for a very long time." Myrna's eyes softened. "I've prayed for Keeton's family. I've prayed for your heart to heal, and to open up to someone special, Sophie." Myrna sniffed. "I've done all of this work praying, so please, at least give God a chance."

"We will." Keeton rubbed his left hand across his jaw. He knew how good Myrna could be at this, and yet he'd fallen right into her trap.

She still looked sympathetic, though. She didn't smile and say, "Gotcha."

Instead she turned to kiss Sophie on the cheek. "Get cleaned up. There's a new restaurant in Grove. Let him take you out to dinner. And don't give me that nonsense about dating bull riders. Look at him, he's getting old. It isn't like he's going to be riding much longer anyway."

"Ouch," he muttered as Myrna fast-walked back to her car. He turned to Sophie. "I knew what to expect, but wow, she's good."

"We're not going out to eat." Sophie smiled and patted his cheek. "She's good. And I'm immune to her skills."

"You have to eat."

"I have cereal and a new carton of milk."

Keeton handed Lucy to Sophie. "I'll let your mule out."

"Thank you." She took his daughter and held her close. "Have you heard from her mother again?"

"No. I've tried to call a few times. No answer."

"I hope she's okay."

He opened the gate wide and the mule trotted out, then ran. He cleared a fence a short distance away and kept going. Keeton shook his head and then he walked back to where Sophie waited.

"She's fine. She's playing some kind of game with me. But I have news for her. I'm not going to give up my daughter." He looked back in the direction the mule had gone. "You're going to have to put up electric fences to keep him in."

"I know." And then her smile disappeared. "I can't imagine you not having Lucy."

"Yeah. You know, a month ago I couldn't have imagined *having* her. Now I can't imagine not. The first day when Becka showed up and pushed her in my arms, I have to admit, I was a little upset. I didn't know what to do with a baby, or how to take care of her. At first I wasn't sure she was mine."

"But she is."

He nodded. "Yeah. I had a DNA test."

"You've done a great job with her, Keeton."

"You've been a big help." He stepped next to Sophie and they walked side by side back to the house. "I should go to town and get Dad some dinner."

"Right. I'm going to pour myself that bowl of cereal."

Keeton took Lucy from her. "I could bring you back something."

For a second he thought she'd say yes, but then she shook her head. "No, thanks. I think I'm going to eat my cereal and go to bed early."

"Right, we wouldn't want Granny Cooper to think she's won."

"Exactly."

She kissed his cheek, and then she kissed Lucy. Keeton watched her walk back to her house and then he turned away. But Myrna's words were still playing in his mind. He laughed, because he guessed that was exactly what she'd planned. But he also guessed it was going to take faith like hers, not his, to convince Sophie to give them a chance.

Chapter Twelve

The next weekend Sophie pulled into the rodeo grounds with a trailer hauling her mule Lucky. Keeton had offered to trailer the animal. But after a thirty-minute talk on why he thought this could be a bad idea, and how she might get hurt, she'd told him she could trailer her own mule.

And then she'd kissed Lucy because who could walk away without kissing Lucy? Even though the action brought her far too close to Keeton. Close enough to smell the spicy scent of his cologne. Close enough to know he chewed cinnamon gum and had dried his clothes on the line behind the guesthouse. Close enough that if she'd tilted her head just a certain way, her lips would almost have touched his neck. All of those things she told herself she didn't want—or need—were more than she could handle at times.

It made it easier to blame her grandmother.

Not that Sophie didn't have ideas of her own, but her grandmother had a way of making everything look perfectly reasonable and like the best idea ever.

Even now she could smell Keeton. She pulled up the collar of her shirt and sure enough, Keeton. She didn't know if she should burn the shirt when she got home, or keep it forever without washing it. Of course, that would be very high school, and she was quite a few years beyond such gestures.

Really.

She stepped out of her truck and walked to the back of the trailer, doing a quick scan of the crowd and looking for Lucky. She spotted him. He'd backed his trailer in next to Jackson's. They were near the portable dance floor where the band would set up after the rodeo. This was Dawson's Summer Fling. All year the planning committee worked on the event. They planned food, music, the parade and the events. Things had kicked off the night before with a showdeo for the younger kids to participate in. Tonight would be the traditional rodeo events.

Lucky and Jackson had brought out their big fifth-wheel trailers that also included living quarters. Normally they would have brought a smaller stock trailer to a local event, but this one sometimes went on late into the night. They were planning on kids needing to sleep, bathroom breaks and a place to get out of the summer heat if necessary.

She unlatched the back of her trailer and let the rear gate swing wide. Lucky—the mule, not the brother—turned to look at her. His big ears twitched and he trembled a little. He'd never been exposed to anything like this.

"Easy, boy. I promise, this will be fun. And I'll take you home as soon as your part in the entertainment is over."

Lucky snorted and lowered his big head. She slid up next to him and rubbed his ears. A cat would have purred. Lucky leaned against her. His big head pushed against her stomach and she scratched his neck.

She untied his lead rope and backed him out of the trailer. His hooves clunked and the wood floor of the trailer rattled. Lucky backed out quickly, his hind hooves hitting firm ground. He shuddered again.

"Looks like you made it." Keeton's voice. She walked out of the trailer and shot him a smile that wasn't quite the real thing.

"Of course I made it."

"I didn't doubt you." He stepped closer.

"Where's Lucy?" She shot a look past him, searching for her brothers.

"My mom and dad are here and they have her."

"They're together?"

He reached for the lead rope but she didn't let him take it.

"Yes, together. Mom came back yesterday. She said she can't leave him like this. She has some vacation time and she knows I can't take care of him and Lucy. I think she's afraid he'll start drinking again."

"How'd the appointment go yesterday, with the lawyer?" She'd talked to them before they took off to Tulsa to discuss what might come of his dad's accident.

"He hopes he can get Dad into a treatment program before they go to court. That would look good to a judge and hopefully he'll just get probation."

"I really hope it works out for him." She held tight to the rope to keep from reaching for Keeton's hand. "I hope it works out for them."

Keeton pushed his hat back and his grin touched secret places in her heart. "Me, too. But they've talked. Mom said she isn't ready to move back here. He isn't ready to leave. They explained that friendship is the best they can do for now."

"It can't be easy for either of them. Or for you?"

"No, it isn't easy." He walked to the back of her truck and pulled out the saddle and bridle.

"Why don't you get him saddled so he has a chance to calm down before this parade?"

"You want to talk me out of this, don't you?"

"I'm not going to try. Just be careful."

She nodded and held the rope while he saddled the mule. She let him do it. He'd done so much for her. He knew when to back off, to not push. And she knew that it was okay to let him take these small steps into her life, because he wouldn't take up everything. He wouldn't take control.

She closed her eyes briefly and Lucky moved, pushing his head against her. She opened her eyes and watched Keeton pull the girth strap tight. The mule held his breath, bloating his stomach. Keeton moved him back a step and pulled again, tightening the strap so the saddle wouldn't slip while she was riding.

"There you go." He handed her the reins. "You're sure he's—"

She held up a hand and stopped him. "He's ready."

"Okay. Let me give you a leg up." If he had more to tell her, he kept it to himself.

Her heart kind of teetered on the brink, filling up, tilting, settling. She looked at him and his smile pushed her heart a little closer to the edge.

The edge? Of being broken again?

He cupped his hands and she put her left foot

up, he held it in his hands. She swung her right leg over the back of the mule, landing lightly in the saddle. Lucky moved to the side but then he settled. She looked down at Keeton and he smiled up at her and tipped his hat in a salute.

"Well done, Soph. Now let's see what your brother thinks of his namesake."

"I can't believe he didn't find out." The moment hit, what she'd done. "I can't believe I'm doing this."

"I can. What are you afraid of?"

"Nothing." She wasn't afraid. "I'm not afraid. Maybe nervous."

His smile shifted and he put a hand on her leg. She looked down, steadying the mule as the animal tried to move forward.

"I'm riding tonight." He held the bridle and looked up at her.

"I know."

"And you aren't going to try and talk me out of it?"

She shrugged, as if it didn't really matter. But it did. She wanted to tell him not to ride. She wanted him to let go of childish dreams and a career that could lead to serious injury.

"You didn't talk me out of riding Lucky."

He smiled and his eyes crinkled at the corners. "No, because I knew I couldn't. It's your decision."

"Riding bulls is your decision, Keeton. I stand

by mine, to not date bull riders. But riding is up to you. I won't be here to watch. I can't."

"Sophie, you need to trust that God is in charge and that He can keep me safe."

She shook her head and her vision swam as tears filled her eyes. "Does that mean He chose not to keep Kade safe?"

"That isn't at all what I meant." He took off his hat and rubbed a hand over his eyes. "Sophie, somewhere along the way we have to learn to trust. Whether it's driving down the road, getting in a plane, facing an illness or riding a bull, we have to trust God. We can't expect life to be pain free, we trust God with every situation and know that whatever happens, He has it under control and He'll get us through."

"Right." She felt his hand on hers, looked down and watched their fingers slide together. "Is bull riding really your dream?"

He shoved his hat back on his head and stepped away from her. "It's what I do."

Sophie wanted his hand back. She wanted to apologize. Deflecting wasn't fair. Making it about him, not her, that hadn't been anywhere close to okay. She tried to apologize but he shook his head.

"It's my dream." He said the words with careful enunciation and walked away.

Good way to push the guy away so he doesn't

get too close, Sophie. She groaned at her lecture to herself, and then turned Lucky in the direction of the arena.

As she rode through the big gate into the freshly plowed arena, she searched the crowd for Lucky. And for Keeton. She spotted Lucky first. She waved and trotted around the arena on the big red mule he'd bought for hunting.

"Hey, that's my mule." He ran to the gate and she knew he'd be waiting for her.

As she rode past she saw Jackson pound Lucky on the back and heard him say, "Looks to me like it's Sophie's mule."

She smiled and saluted her brother. It didn't happen very often, that she kept something from Clan Cooper, but this time she'd done it.

Out of the corner of her eye she saw Keeton move. She turned and he nodded once and walked away. Yes, she'd really done it.

Keeton headed for the bull pen to stretch and get warmed up for his ride. There were several events beforehand, so he had a long while to wait. From behind the scenes he watched Sophie lead the mule back to her trailer. Lucky, the brother, walked with her. He laughed on occasion and patted her on the back. She smiled up at him.

Well played, Sophie. Keeton smiled as he raised

his arms and leaned left, then right. He did that several times, and then he held his arms out and made big circles to loosen his shoulder muscles. A few other riders, most way younger than him, gathered around to join him in some deep knee bends.

"Hey, Keeton, how do you stay in shape?" A young rider, probably just out of high school, twisted at the torso as he asked the question.

"I work out a few days a week." Keeton reached forward and took some deep breaths. "I lift weights."

"And chase pretty girls." Another of the younger Coopers, Dylan, laughed as he made the statement.

Keeton smiled and shook his head. He shoved his hat down tight and reached to buckle his chaps. "My girl-chasing days are long gone. I'll leave that to you younger guys."

"Oh, come on, you know you're after a world title and my sister." Dylan grunted as he leaned forward, back and then side to side. "She must be pretty interested, 'cause she didn't leave and she always leaves."

"She's a Cooper, Dylan, of course she's staying for the rodeo."

"No, she usually leaves before bull riding."

Keeton didn't want to have this conversation with a group of kids that were barely out of school.

"You gonna win the world title this year?" a kid with straw-colored hair and a big smile asked.

"I'm going to try." Keeton pulled a glove out of his pocket.

Next to the fence of the arena he spotted Sophie. She stood next to her sister Heather. The two of them appeared to be sharing a story. She hadn't left. He wondered if that meant she'd decided to trust God. Or had she lost track of time?

Her words to him slipped through his mind again. Was this his dream, or Kade's? The truth kind of hurt. He'd been riding bulls for the better part of sixteen years because right after Kade died, Keeton had decided to win the world title for his little brother. And it hadn't happened. The years had slipped by, he'd made some good money riding, and he hadn't quit.

He hadn't accomplished much more than riding bulls and trying to win a title he'd never really cared about.

He shuffled in the dirt a little as he walked away from the kids still warming up. He kind of wanted to kick himself, because Sophie was right. Man, she was right. Not that he had any intention of letting her know.

As right as she was, he had to get his mind back on riding. Tonight he was riding a bull Jackson kept bragging about. And in two weeks he planned on making an event in Texas. He was still chasing that dream. It occurred to him that he had a hard time letting go.

His attention shot to Sophie. Yeah, he had a real hard time letting go. Over the years he'd thought about her a lot. Wondered if things could have been different. But things weren't and she had loved his little brother. He also wondered if she still loved Kade, or was it the memory, the dream of what they might have had that she loved?

Or had she let go and just got stuck, like him?

After team roping came bull riding. Keeton jerked his focus back to the task at hand. He couldn't let his mind wander when a one-ton animal wanted nothing more than to pound his sorry hide into the ground.

As he waited his turn outside the chutes he thought about a question a reporter had once asked. What made a guy want to ride a bull? He had laughed it off back then, because he'd been a lot younger. He'd come in second that year, winning finals, but not the title. He'd said something stupid about women. But what did make a guy want to ride a bull? Adrenaline? The ability to overcome fear or to conquer? Money?

They called his name and he headed for the chutes. Jackson grinned and pointed to a big Brahma-cross bull that he'd recently bought.

"Keeton West, you're about to take the ride of your life."

"Shucks, Jackson, that bull ain't no bigger than a pony I rode when I was about six years old."

Jackson laughed and took Keeton's bull rope. "Let me help you get strapped in."

Keeton felt a sharp pain and he drew in a breath. His mind fogged a little and his memory took him on a wild ride, back in time. He was nineteen, standing where Jackson stood. His brother had drawn one of the meanest bulls around. They were right here, in this same spot.

And he hadn't ridden here since then. Not once. His parents hadn't sat on the bleachers of this arena since that night. Sounded as though Sophie hadn't, either.

He stood on the catwalk and searched the crowd. He spotted her standing at the edge of the arena, not sitting. He knew she wouldn't sit. She'd want to be able to walk away, to not watch.

Not too long ago he'd told her to trust. Trust.

What in the world was he doing? At his age, he should have a wife and kids. He should have a job that he went to every day. He should take Jeremy up on that offer to help run the bigger facility he planned for Dawson, building custom bikes.

"Keet, you okay?" Jackson cleared his throat. "Hey, you know you don't have to do this, right?"

"I know." He eased himself over the side of the chute, and then situated himself on the back of the bull. "But I'm going to ride this bull that hasn't been ridden. By the time I get done with him, he'll be as tame as that mule of Sophie's."

"Big talk." Jackson grinned and pulled the bull rope tight. The rope was wrapped around the big animal belly. Keeton had rosined up his gloved hand to keep the rope sticky and in place. He wrapped it tight, holding his hand to the bull, to the rope situated at the base of the bull's neck.

The bull leaned against the side of the chute, pushing his bad knee against the gate. He grimaced and breathed deep, forgetting the pain. Jackson held his vest to keep him steady in case the bull decided to pitch him forward. More than one guy had lost a tooth or even cracked a jaw after being thrown forward.

He'd seen guys hauled out of the chute unconscious. Why did a guy do this? A question for the ages.

The bull settled and he had his thoughts back on track just in time. He nodded once and the gate shot open. The bull spun like a maniac, flying into the arena, all four hooves off the ground at once. He leaned forward, steadying himself. The jarring force of hitting the ground knocked him to the left side of the bull, and then the crazy animal switched directions on him, the way Keeton had been warned he'd do. Keeton leaned the other direction to keep from spiraling down on the inside of the spin.

He looked up, saw Sophie for just a flash as the bull spun. Eight seconds seemed like eight minutes. He broke at the hips, pushing forward when the bull jumped and tried to get him off his back.

The buzzer rang. He unwrapped his hand, realized it had been loose the whole time. Travis Cooper stood nearby, yelling, telling him to wait. Travis moved, got the bull turning toward him. Keeton jumped, landed, stumbled back. The bull turned, bellowed, ran.

Travis jumped in front of the bull, then jumped, nearly doing a cartwheel off the animal's big head. Yeah, bull fighters were athletes. And lifesavers.

The bull lost interest and headed for the gate that opened for him to run out, back to the pen. Travis leaned, resting his hands on his knees. He took a deep breath and then straightened. Travis grinned big and walked past him.

"Saved your hide, now, didn't I?"

"Travis, you're my hero."

Travis slapped him on the back. "You're not my brother's hero. You just rode his unridable bull. And I think, from the look on her face, you're not Sophie's hero."

"I'll make it up to them both."

Keeton walked out of the arena. Sophie had remained close to the gate. He smiled as he approached her. She shook her head and he noticed tears streaming down her cheeks.

"It's over."

"No, it isn't." She walked away and he let her go because he knew Sophie. He knew she'd need a minute. She wouldn't want to cry in front of people. She wouldn't want everyone to know her business.

For now he'd go check on his parents. And Lucy. He breathed deep and shook out the catch in his leg, in his bad knee. He exhaled past the moment, thinking maybe they'd all needed this ride. He, his parents and Sophie.

Maybe they needed this moment to conquer what the past had done to them? Maybe now they could all rebuild what had been broken inside them when Kade died?

Chapter Thirteen

Sophie spent the rest of the rodeo talking to Lucky—the mule, not her brother. Lucky the mule didn't talk back or tell her what to think or explain that her emotions were all over the place. Lucky just listened.

God listened. She leaned against the mule's neck and told God that she didn't know what to do with her feelings, with her pain, with her fear. And she realized it had already been summed up in that one word Keeton had said earlier. *Trust*.

Trust that God knew His plan for her life, and she should know that it would be the best thing for her. Trust that God knew how things were going to work out, even when she didn't.

Lean not unto your own understanding.

While Keeton had been riding that bull, she'd done a lot of trusting. She'd had to block a lot of images. And she'd stood her ground, faced her fear.

It had felt pretty good. And then adrenaline had evaporated and she'd felt nothing but shaky and weak.

In the distance she could hear the band setting up. She led Lucky to the trailer and he stepped inside as if he'd been trailered his whole young life. Not once had she ever wanted a mule. Never. She'd grown up riding some of the best quarter horses in the country. But Lucky the mule kind of changed things for her.

She smiled at that thought. Once again she'd found her thing.

"What's that smile for?"

She turned and smiled at Keeton. In the distance she heard the band singing a country song about taking chances. They could leave here the way they came. Or they could see what might happen if they took a chance on each other.

"That smile is because I've found what I love."

"Me?"

She laughed and then ignored his statement. "I love mules. All my life I've had quarter horses, like a good, respectable Cooper. But I now know that I love mules. I think I might buy more."

"Stop the presses." He reached for her hands and pulled her close. "Sophie Cooper is a mule person."

"I know." She smiled because it came easy,

smiling in his arms, being held by him as they swayed to music in the distance.

"What do we do, Sophie? Do we take a chance? Do we walk away and always wonder? Do we stay friends or see what will happen with us? Forget who we thought we were going to be and see who we can become?"

They were swaying to lyrics similar to what he said, and she thought about it, about jumping in and not regretting. He leaned, nuzzling her neck, holding her close. He smelled a little like the rodeo and a lot like Keeton. She could feel his heart beating close to her chin as she rested her head on his shoulder.

"I want to." She looked up. Unsure. Unsteady. "I want to see what happens."

He leaned and she closed her eyes. Swept away by the moment she forgot where they were. She didn't care who saw. She didn't think about what people might say or who they might tell.

His lips were warm on hers and she wanted nothing more than to be in his arms, feeling him hold her tight. She moved her hands from his shoulders to his neck. Yes, her grandmother had always warned her that dancing could lead to necking. She smiled at the thought and Keeton whispered her name, whispered words she didn't hear.

Sirens ripped through the night. They pulled

back from each other, looked toward the crowd that had gathered around the makeshift dance floor. The band stopped playing and someone shouted for Jackson.

"We need to see what's going on." Keeton held her hand and they headed back toward the arena.

Sophie couldn't think about what might be happening. She couldn't stop thinking about the declaration they'd just made and how they'd deal with it tomorrow, when it wasn't a moonlit night with stars twinkling in a velvety dark sky and the scent of honeysuckle in the air.

Tomorrow when it was broad daylight and reality couldn't be ignored.

Reality. As they got closer to the crowd, Jackson spotted them and hurried in their direction. Sickening dread welled up inside Sophie as her brother got closer. Keeton's hand tightened on hers.

"It's nothing," he assured her as they stopped and waited for Jackson.

"Nothing?" Sophie looked up at him. "It's something or Jackson wouldn't be looking for me. It's the houses, again. Why?"

"You don't know that's what it is."

"Don't I?

Jackson had been followed by his daughter, Jade. "Soph, the call is for your place."

Her place? All of the air left her lungs and the

world became a blur. Keeton told her to take a deep breath. She couldn't. Jade had thrown her arms around Sophie.

"The barn, Sophie, your barn," Jackson repeated until the words cleared her mind and made sense.

Thirty seconds had passed. She breathed in and out, Keeton's hand on hers. Jade holding her tight. Why? Who would be so against a few houses that they'd set fire to her barn?

"We should go." Keeton had slid his arm around her waist. "I'll drive you."

"Lucky." Her mule.

"Travis can take him to the main barn." Jackson put his fingers in the corners of his mouth, whistled loud and waved for Travis to head their way.

"Okay."

She needed to take charge, make decisions.

Jackson's radio blasted and someone on the end said they were on scene, the barn was engulfed but they'd control it and protect the main house. Sophie wiped at her eyes.

"Let's go." Jackson shot Keeton a look. "Drive her. I'm heading that way."

A few minutes later they were in the truck. Keeton glanced at her and she shrugged and looked out the window of the truck into the dark night. Ahead she could see the orange glow of fire against the dark night sky.

"I just don't get it," she whispered and then she covered her eyes and thought, prayed. "I'm so sorry you had to leave Lucy with your parents."

"They really don't mind. And I want to be with you."

"Thank you." They slowed to turn on the road that led to her house. Now she could see the flames. There were flickering lights from emergency vehicles, bright headlights and people everywhere.

"The police are here," Keeton announced and she nodded. She saw the police cars.

"My quiet, anonymous life." She shook her head. "Why did I think this would be easy? I thought I'd be able to build these houses, no one would ever know it was me. I never thought someone would want to stop me."

He kind of laughed, and she looked at him. He gave her a half smile, an apologetic look. "You thought no one would know?"

"Yeah, I did."

"Why does it matter?"

It was her turn to shrug. "I guess it doesn't. It used to, but now it doesn't seem to be that important."

They got out of the truck and walked toward the barn, toward emergency vehicles, firemen, police officers. Someone really wanted to stop her from building those houses. They wanted it stopped so badly they were willing to torch her barn.

A police officer approached. She didn't know him but he smiled and looked from Keeton to her. "Ms. Cooper, I have to ask you a few questions."

"Of course." She wished she had answers.

The questioning lasted for thirty minutes. And at one point she started to ask him if she was a suspect. She looked at Keeton and he must have known because he shook his head. Okay, fine, she wasn't going to ask.

Out of the blue came the question she hadn't expected. "Do you know the Gordons?"

"Of course I do."

"Have they said anything to you about this property, contacted you in any way?"

"We've talked. I offered to help them and even offered them a portion of the land I bought. They didn't want it. They're older and want to live in town. Mr. Gordon is working as a manager at one of our apartment complexes."

"I see. Did you know their nephew is volunteering at your development?" The officer continued to write in his notebook.

"Yes, I knew that. He's out of work and wanted to help friends."

"Okay, that's all I need for now. I'm really sorry about this, Ms. Cooper. And I do want to warn you to be cautious until we can make an arrest."

"Okay, I will."

Keeton held her close and she didn't know what to think. She leaned against him, but leaning on him seemed wrong. What would she have done had he not been here to turn to? She would have driven herself. She would have taken Lucky to her parents' house and she would have dealt with this situation.

Good or bad? She didn't know, not right then.

"I have to go talk to Jackson." She pulled away from Keeton's side.

"Do you want me to go?"

She shook her head. "No, you need to go get Lucy. I'm good. I can handle this."

"I know you can. But if you want me here…"

"I'm good." Stubborn. Strong willed. Afraid to rely on him too much.

Before he walked away he leaned and kissed her cheek. "Call me if you need anything. And don't be afraid to need a friend. I'm not here to take over. I'm just here."

She nodded and before he could step away she touched his cheek and allowed herself a good-bye kiss.

* * *

Keeton drove to Myrna Cooper's where he found his parents sitting in the lamp-lit living room. They were sitting side by side on the sofa, his mom was holding Lucy. They looked up and smiled when he walked through the door.

"How's Sophie?" his mom asked.

"She's good. The barn is a complete loss but her house is okay."

His mom stood and handed Lucy to him. "She's missed you, I think. And I wasn't asking about Sophie's barn. Tonight couldn't have been easy for her."

"Was it easy for any of us?" Keeton sat down on a rocking chair and gave a push with his foot to set it in motion. Lucy rested in the crook of his arm.

His dad looked at his mom. She finally spoke. "It wasn't easy but I think I needed to do that. I needed to face my fears."

"We all have to do that from time to time." He smiled down at his daughter with her drooling, lopsided baby grin. He'd dressed her in a denim romper and little boots for the rodeo. His mom had changed her into a sleeper covered with pink lambs.

His lawyer had called the other day and said he'd gotten a letter from an attorney representing

Becka. She wanted visitation rights. It wouldn't be easy, letting her see their daughter, but he'd do it. If it meant he got to keep Lucy, he'd do it.

"Keeton, we've all suffered," his mom started. "I won't regret or feel guilty for what I did. I couldn't stay here with the memories."

"Mom, I know that."

"I want to apologize. I could have done things differently. You shouldn't have to buy back land that would have been yours."

"I've only bought twenty acres."

"Is there any way to get the rest?" his dad asked.

"No, there isn't. Sophie bought part. I think a hunting lodge bought the rest."

"We could try." His mom looked sincere as she made the offer. "I could help. There are rental houses from the money we walked away with. I could sell some of our rental houses and free up some cash."

Buy it all back. He leaned back and continued to rock Lucy. She closed her eyes, opened them, closed them again. Her little hand came up and found his collar. This had become the nightly sleeping ritual and he smiled because he had gotten as used to it as she had. Finally he shook his head in answer to her question.

Six months ago he'd wanted all of the land. Having it had been the most important thing to him. Now it didn't matter. He shrugged. "I don't need it all."

Having all of the land wouldn't make his family whole. The land wouldn't fix what had been broken. He looked at Lucy, then at his parents. Time had a way of taking care of broken things, mending them. He thought about scabs he'd had as a kid. His mom would tell him to leave it alone, don't pick at it, let it heal.

He'd done a whole lot of picking after Kade's death. He'd done a lot of his own blaming. He'd blamed his mom for his dad's alcoholism. He'd blamed his dad for not being strong enough to hold on to his family and his land. He'd blamed himself.

He'd picked and picked, and then he'd let it go and let it heal up. Looking at his parents he saw something he hadn't seen in a long, long time. He saw a family. Even if they didn't get back together, his parents could be grandparents to Lucy, they could be friends.

Funny how circumstances had brought them all here together at the same time. Funny? He looked up and said a quick, silent thank-you.

But what about Sophie? Where did she fit in this grand plan? He kind of hoped she fit in his life, the way he'd thought she might, even years ago.

Convincing Sophie to give them a shot might

be a whole new challenge. He'd felt her lose herself in his arms tonight. She'd let go of some fears. And then she'd pushed him away.

Because? He thought he knew why. Because she needed to be in charge of her life, not consumed by people. Or even by him. He had grown up in a quiet house with a younger brother and two parents who had given them plenty of space.

Life as a Cooper would have been a whole lot different. Life as a Cooper would have meant always having someone involved. He remembered as kids, Jackson had always been the brother tailing Sophie, getting in her business, involving himself if he thought she needed help. Blake had been almost as bad.

Once, years ago, she'd had a flat tire. He'd stopped to help fix it. She'd told him she could do it herself. And five minutes later, as he stood there watching, letting her do it, her brother Blake showed up. He took the jack and the tire iron and changed the tire, ignoring her protests that she could have done it herself.

He grinned and thought he might remind her of that. He hadn't tried to change that tire. He'd known full well that she could do it herself.

"I should head home." He stood up with his sleeping daughter in his arms. It wasn't an easy maneuver with a bad knee and Lucy sound asleep. He managed, though, and he didn't fall or break anything. His dad stood, hobbling on his new walking cast. That must mean they were leaving together.

"I'll go, too." His dad looked down at Keeton's mom and she smiled a little. "Take care, Doris."

"I'll see you in a few days, James. We'll find a good program."

His dad turned a little red and cleared his throat. Men like his dad were used to handling things. They didn't get counseling, treatment, or really ever admit they had a problem. Sometimes that worked for them. Sometimes it all fell apart.

"That'll be good." His dad limped to the front door of the house. "I appreciate it."

Keeton's mom followed them to the door. "It's been a long time, but I think the one thing we've learned in the last few weeks is that we're still a family. We've had a lot of time and distance between us, but we can still be there."

Keeton kissed her cheek and walked down the steps. He was buckling Lucy into the car seat when his dad hobbled up.

"Doing okay, Dad?"

"Yeah, guess so. I guess there's something to talking things out. Maybe we should have talked after…after Kade…"

"After he died?" Keeton turned and his dad was leaning against the side of the truck looking up at the sky.

"Yeah, we should have talked. I should have asked you how you were doing."

"I don't know if I would have answered."

"Maybe not, but I should have asked." His dad looked at him now. "How you doin', son? Now, I mean."

"I'm doing good, Dad. I've been good for a long time. I felt guilty for a long time. I was pretty angry with you, and with Mom. But I was a kid and that's what a kid does. And then I just settled with my life, got my degree and rode bulls."

"But you missed living here."

"Well, yeah, I did. We're talking like I'm sixteen, not thirty-six."

His dad laughed a little. "Guess I'm late to the game. We should have had this conversation years ago."

"Probably so. Now it's just time to let it go and move on."

"But you're okay?"

Keeton walked around the front of the truck and got in on the driver's side. He closed the door and started the engine as his dad climbed in on the other side.

"Dad, I'm good."

"You going to marry Sophie Cooper?"

"I haven't gotten that far into the plan."

"Seems like a good fit." His dad leaned back in the seat and closed his eyes. "I think Kade…"

Keeton nearly closed his eyes, but he caught himself. "Dad, don't."

The last thing Keeton needed to feel like was a replacement. He'd walked away from Sophie years earlier because that's what he would have been.

He'd told her that night, the night after Kade's funeral, that he wanted to be in her life but he wasn't going to stay and be a replacement, the guy she settled with.

He'd been young. She'd been heartbroken. It had been a kid thing to do and say. She'd cried and probably called him a few names he deserved.

Looking back he realized he'd done them both a favor. If they'd stayed in each other's lives back then, they might not have survived the emotions. One or both of them would have questioned why they were together.

After all of these years, if they gave this a chance, they would know it was real, not leftover feelings. Not Keeton coming in second.

Chapter Fourteen

On Monday Sophie stood in the yard looking at what used to be her barn. A pile of charred lumber and blackened tin that used to be the roof was all that she had left of a structure built nearly one hundred years earlier. In her arms, Lucy fussed and chewed on her fist. The baby gave up on the fist and rubbed her mouth on Sophie's shoulder.

"Teething or hungry?" she whispered to Lucy and kissed the baby's soft head. "We'll go inside and get a nice bottle of formula. Maybe you need a nap."

She'd volunteered to watch Sophie when Keeton had left the previous day to take his dad to Tulsa. An opening had come available in a treatment program. In-house for a month. She prayed it would get James West back on track. She'd been praying for Keeton's parents to reunite. She smiled at the thought. A couple that obviously still loved each other should be together. She thought that after all of these years, the fact that they were both still single said a lot.

So why was she still single? One last look at the barn and she turned toward the house, shutting out thoughts that would clearly just get her down. Especially with a sweet reminder of what she'd missed cradled in her arms. Silly, but she'd spent a lot of years thinking she'd never find the right guy.

The dates she'd been on had left her thinking there had to be something more. She wanted something that felt like it should last forever, not something that might be fun for a date or two. She wanted a man in her life whom she wanted to spend time with.

She'd been spending a lot of time with Keeton.

The thought brought a sigh. Lucy smiled up at her, the fist back in her rosebud mouth. "Lucy, this is worse than talking to myself. I'm having conversations in my mind. This is the first step to being an old maid, I know it is."

Lucy cooed very sweetly and Sophie thought that in baby talk the infant must be telling her to "get a life."

A car turned into her driveway. Sophie had made it to her back door but she stopped and waited to see who would get out of the old truck. When the Gordons stepped out, she smiled and waved.

But why were they here? She figured she would have her chance to ask them that in a few minutes. Mr. Gordon waited at the front of the truck for his wife and they both walked up, easily reaching for each other, holding hands.

Even at their age. Sophie wanted to know how a person got that. Everyone seemed to be able to find it but her.

"Mr. and Mrs. Gordon! It's great to see the two of you." In the back of her mind she remembered the police officer's questions the night the barn caught fire. She felt a moment's hesitation and brushed it aside.

"Good to see you, too, Ms. Cooper." Mr. Gordon led his wife across uneven ground and then up the path to where Sophie stood. Mrs. Gordon touched a rose bloom as she passed the bush at the edge of the patio.

"Lovely flowers, Sophie. I used to—" and then she smiled a tight smile "—I used to grow roses. But we've planted new bushes at the corner of our apartment. Chuck even put a garden at the edge of the apartment complex. Several of the tenants are working on it together."

"I love to hear that, Mrs. Gordon. Is there something I can do for the two of you?"

"Well, we're afraid we have news that you need." Mr. Gordon looked at his wife and then back to Sophie. "About the fires."

Sophie pointed to the patio table. "Let's sit down. Could I get either of you anything? Coffee, iced tea?"

"No, nothing for us. We just came from the Mad Cow. We can't go without Vera's fried chicken so we come over to Dawson every Monday for the lunch special."

Half the county drove to Dawson for Vera's fried chicken. But the Gordon's serious expression kept Sophie from mentioning the chicken.

"You heard about the fires?" Sophie waited for them to sit at the patio table and she sat across from them, still cuddling a now-fussy Lucy. "Would you mind if I get her a bottle?"

"No, of course not." Mrs. Gordon smiled. "Is she a niece?"

"She's Keeton West's daughter. I'm watching her for a couple of days."

"We heard about his house."

Sophie nodded as she stood. "The police don't believe the fires are related. I'll be right back."

When she returned, Lucy had her bottle and Sophie had a growing sense of unease. She sat down again, holding the bottle as Lucy made noisy sucking sounds.

"We're afraid that our nephew has something

to do with this vandalism." Mr. Gordon pushed a hand through thinning gray hair. "I hope that's not the truth, but if he's doing this, then he needs to be stopped."

Sophie leaned forward, turning a little in her chair to make room for Lucy in her arms. Her heart ached for the Gordons, for all they'd lost and the way they'd managed to keep going.

"Why do you think Gabe would do this? He's been helping me build the houses."

"He's bitter, Sophie. Some people just let bitterness get to them. We didn't have kids of our own. I guess he always thought he'd get that land."

"I'm so sorry. I didn't know." That they hadn't had children, or that their nephew had laid claim to what had been theirs.

"We tried to tell him how much you've done for us. But last night he came to our house ranting and raving about how we'd let him down."

"I think we should call the police." Sophie reached for her cell phone. "I can live with losing a barn. But I wouldn't want him to hurt either of you."

"He isn't like he used to be. He used to be a real good boy. He helped us a lot on the farm." Mrs. Gordon shook her head and a few tears trickled down her cheeks. She pulled a tissue from her purse and wiped them away. "It's a sad world we're living in."

"Getting sadder by the day." Mr. Gordon nodded in affirmation.

And Sophie wondered. Because she heard often that it was a sad world with people not really caring about others. But she'd seen the opposite in the past few weeks. She'd seen a community come together. Even in the past few years with hard times falling on everyone. There were bad people, but she'd seen quite a few good ones, too.

It seemed the bad took the focus off the good.

"Please, don't call the police. Not yet. Let us have a chance to talk to him. If he did do this, maybe we can talk him into turning himself in." Mrs. Gordon twisted her tissue in her hands and looked up with eyes that pleaded for understanding.

"I'm not sure what to do." She'd thought building the housing development would be easy. People helping each other achieve something they couldn't achieve on their own. What could be better?

It only took one angry person to ruin it for everyone.

"We want you to be real careful until this gets hammered out." Mr. Gordon stood and his wife followed. "We'll talk to him tonight."

"Thank you." Sophie watched them go and she wasn't sure what to say or what to do. She definitely didn't think they could talk their nephew into turning himself in. Not if he was as angry as they said.

They drove away and she went inside. And for the first time in a very long time, she locked the deadbolt.

Lucy slept soundly for the next two hours. And Sophie dozed with her. The two of them were curled up on the couch when the doorbell rang. Lucy cried out and Sophie sat up, brushing a hand through her hair. Her heart beat a little faster than normal and she froze, waiting.

"Sophie, it's Keeton."

She stood, leaving Lucy on the couch. The baby had fallen back to sleep, her breathing steady and sure. Sophie pushed the ottoman up against the sofa and rolled a blanket next to the baby to keep her from moving close to the edge.

"Coming," she whispered. "Hold your horses."

She opened the door, and Keeton smiled and held out a dozen roses. The fragrance greeted her, his smile greeted her. She took the flowers and motioned him inside, a finger to her lips.

"How's my girl?" He peeked around the corner and smiled when he saw his daughter. "She looks pretty happy."

Sophie smiled because Lucy had woken up

and she had her feet up, playing with her toes. "She's been a very good girl."

He took off his hat and hung it on the hook next to her front door. Then he kicked off his boots. Sophie watched him looking so at home, so comfortable in her world. Before she could move away with the flowers, his arm snaked around her waist and he pulled her close.

"I missed you." His cheek brushed hers, rough and masculine. He touched her cheek and turned her to settle his lips on hers. "We have unfinished business."

Do we? she wanted to ask. But she couldn't think straight, not with his hands on her waist, his lips on hers. *Think back,* she told herself, *to what could have been.*

A lifetime with this man. The thought jarred her from the moment and she stepped back.

"How's your dad?"

Keeton grinned. "Good. He's going to be good."

"I'm glad to hear that. Would you like coffee?"

"Not really." He glanced at his watch. "Do you have food in this house or should I take you out to dinner?"

"I happen to have food. I went to the store after church yesterday and bought real food."

"Real food? We're not going to be subjected to toaster pastries for dinner?"

"Only if you keep mocking me." She slipped

away from his touch and from the teasing voice that belonged to her heart, the one that kept asking her why she was running from something that could be the most perfect thing to ever happen to her.

Keeton let Sophie walk away. She hurried down the hall to the kitchen and he smiled at how quickly she had to get away from him, and probably away from what she felt. He kind of liked knowing that she at least felt something in his arms. Nothing hurt a guy's ego worse than lack of interest.

His baby girl had fallen back to sleep. He wanted to pick her up and tell her they'd survive anything, together. Even her mother. Yeah, they'd survive Becka trying to get custody. Four months ago when his little girl had been born, he hadn't had a clue about her existence. Now that he knew her, he wouldn't stop fighting to keep her in his life. He definitely wouldn't give her back to the mom who had dumped her.

When he walked into the kitchen a few minutes later, Sophie turned. She smiled a hesitant smile and went back to cutting chicken and vegetables into chunks.

"Kebabs?" She opened a drawer and pulled out sticks.

"Sounds good." He leaned on the counter and watched. "You okay?"

She nodded and kept working. Chicken, zucchini, peppers, chunks of onions. He grabbed damp skewers from a tray and started pushing the meat and vegetables on. She continued to cut.

"The Gordons came by. They think it's Gabe."

"Gabe?" He paused midpush with a chunk of pineapple in his hand.

"Setting the fires."

"Why do they think that?"

"He stopped by their apartment and said a few things that concerned them. They want to talk to him before I call the police. I don't know if that's the right thing to do. What if he does something else before they can talk to him?"

"Soph, if you're harboring any thoughts of talking to this guy, I want you to leave it alone. Call the police but don't you go near him."

She looked up, her brows arched, and he knew he'd said the wrong thing. "You want me to leave it alone?"

"I could have said that better." He looked down at the stick filled with meat and vegetables and he tried hard not to smile.

"I should have said, 'We should let the police handle this.'"

"Good save." She picked up a stick and he

backed away. "Do not start bossing me around like I'm the little lady that you have to protect."

"I kind of like being the man who protects you."

She poked him in the chest with her finger. "I'm very capable of taking care of myself."

"I only meant that I wouldn't want you hurt."

She poked him again, but she smiled. "You're a he-man woman protector."

He chose the next grin to be a little flirty, to soften her up. Always good to fall back on charm, he thought. "I'm a he-man woman protector and I love you."

She shook her head. "No, you don't."

"Yes, I do." He walked over to the sink and washed chicken off his hands. When he turned, she had gone back to cutting meat. The knife in her hands looked a little dangerous.

"Is that such a bad thing, to be loved?"

"No, it isn't bad. It's just not what I expected."

"Really, Sophie? It isn't what you expected?" Man, he'd never been so frustrated by a woman in his life. Maybe because he'd never met one before that made him want to invest everything into a relationship.

"I don't know, Keeton. Maybe I did expect it. Maybe I thought it would work itself out and we'd keep being friends."

"Can't I love you and be your friend? Seems

like the perfect way to have a relationship, if you ask me."

"I wasn't asking you." She finished cutting up their dinner and he started to get the sneaking suspicion that if he kept going on this track, he'd derail and end up eating chicken at the Mad Cow.

"Sophie, I love you." He said it strong and without hesitation. "I'm not going to apologize for loving you. The other night we were dancing and I kind of thought you might feel the same way."

"Moonlight, dancing, kissing, that's what happened between us the other night."

"What are you so afraid of?" He stepped close and he wanted to hold her, but he had a pretty good idea that if he reached for her, she'd punch him.

"I'm not afraid." She shook as she exhaled. "I want to keep things simple."

"Because simple means less invested. Safe." He ran a hand down her arm and touched her hand. "I think I've loved you for years."

"You left." She opened her mouth and then shook her head as if those weren't the words she'd planned.

And maybe they finally had the truth. "I left?"

She closed her eyes. "You walked away. You didn't come back. You went off to chase Kade's dream and you left."

"I left." He was thirty-six years old and blind-sided by something he'd never given a second thought, other than to wonder what might have happened if.

He reached for her but she pulled away and he saw in her eyes that something more was going on. Her eyes looked wild with hurt, with loss.

"Sophie?" He didn't reach for her. "I didn't know you wanted me to stay."

"I had a miscarriage." The words were whispered and her arms wrapped around her middle. She didn't look at him. She'd been strong forever and now he saw that she was strong because it held her together. And he hadn't known.

"I didn't know."

She shook all over, and he didn't know what to do. "No one knew. How could I tell something like that? I definitely couldn't tell my parents and break their hearts."

"I think they—"

She raised her hand to stop him. "I know that now. But as a kid, I thought I couldn't tell them. I thought it would break their hearts if they knew I'd done something like that."

"So what did you do?"

"A friend took me to the doctor, and then I stayed at her house in Grove for a few days, until I could get my head on straight and stop crying."

She wiped her tears with the back of her hand and looked at him.

"Oh, Soph, I'm sorry."

"I was going to have Kade's baby." She shook her head and turned from him when he tried to reach for her.

"Sophie, I'm here now."

She turned, her face pale, her hands shaking. "I know you're here now. But I needed you then. I needed my friend and until you moved, you avoided me. I really wish we weren't having this conversation now. I'm not seventeen. I'm not even twenty-seven."

He owed her an explanation. Now, looking back, he realized he'd made some serious mistakes. After Kade's funeral he'd put distance between himself and Sophie.

"I wanted to give you space."

She looked up, her eyes rimmed with red, tears still hovering on the surface. "Space? When we needed each other, you thought I needed space?"

"I didn't want to be a replacement for Kade. I didn't want to spend my life wondering if you loved me or if I was a replacement for him. I still don't want that to be between us."

The words fell harsh and real between them. He backed up, his hands up in surrender. From the living room he heard Lucy fussing. Reality in diapers.

"You should go." Sophie wiped at her eyes. "We shouldn't have had this conversation and I would appreciate it if you wouldn't tell anyone."

"You think I'd tell?"

"I don't know what I think. I just know that I've made mistakes in my life and I've lived with them."

"And punished yourself for them?"

"Maybe."

"We'll talk tomorrow."

"I don't think I'll be ready to talk tomorrow." She reached into the cabinet for a pan and swiped the food onto it with the knife. She covered it with foil. "I need time."

"I'll give you time, but I'm not walking away from this. We're going to talk. We're going to find a way to move past what happened."

She looked up at the ceiling. Her eyes were dark with shadows and her lips pursed together. He wanted to hold her, but he knew better. He knew she needed time to pull herself together and decide what she wanted.

As he walked out he wondered if he was making another mistake by walking away. Years ago he'd given her space. And that space had now opened into a giant chasm that left them on two sides of a huge canyon.

Chapter Fifteen

Sophie wandered out to pet her mule a few days later. She'd been holed up inside her house, rethinking what she'd told Keeton and wondering why in the world she'd told him. All these years, only her friend Alicia had known. It had been safer that way. At seventeen she'd really thought the whole world would condemn her and paint a scarlet letter on her chest.

She'd messed up. She and Kade had made a big mistake. They'd taken wrong turns and gone places they shouldn't have gone. She had always known that there was a point at which it was hard to return to what was right. She knew the point. Her parents had talked to her about temptation, about knowing where lines are that shouldn't be crossed.

She'd learned the hard way about consequences. A double tragedy, weeks apart.

When people had seen her tears, they'd assumed it all had to do with losing Kade. She now thought it must have been a triple tragedy. She and Keeton had been friends for years and after holding her, kissing her, he'd walked away. He'd told her that night he couldn't take the guilt. He'd put his brother on that bull. And then he'd held Sophie.

Looking back she realized they'd been kids, just kids dealing with very adult situations and not turning to the adults who could have helped them. She should have been more open with her parents. Instead she'd pushed them away. For several long years she pushed everyone away.

The miscarriage and Keeton had become more secrets, things she tried to deal with on her own because she knew that in her family and in a town as small as Dawson, word had a way of getting around.

She should talk to her mom. Now, years too late, she should talk to her about what happened. She poured grain in the feeder for Lucky and swiped a hand down his neck. "See you later, friend."

When she turned, Keeton stood behind her. He held Lucy in her car seat and a backpack was slung over his shoulder.

"Going somewhere?" She focused on Lucy

rather than his haggard expression and the dark shadow of whiskers on his cheeks.

"Yeah, to Broken Arrow. I've got rides to make in the next few weeks and the guy watching my cattle called to tell me he has to go to a funeral."

"So this is goodbye." She didn't want to compare it to the last time they said goodbye, but her mind went back, snagging hold of those memories.

"No, this isn't goodbye. I'll be back and we're going to talk."

"Okay."

"Soph, I'm not going to force myself into your life. I'm too old for that. Either there's something between us that we need to explore, or there isn't."

"I know the one thing I can't do, Keeton. I can't handle the thought of you chasing a dream that isn't yours and putting your life at risk."

"I've been chasing it too long to let go now, Sophie."

"Good luck, then. Be safe."

He tipped his hat and smiled a little. "Will do."

As she stood there trying to figure out what she'd done wrong and how to fix it, he walked back to his truck, buckled Lucy in and then he was gone. She watched his truck until it was out of sight.

Fifteen minutes later she pulled up to her parents' house. Her mom was in the garden. She turned to wave and then went back to weeding tomato plants. Sophie parked and walked to where her mother still worked. The tomato plants were blooming and had small, green tomatoes. The squash plants were spreading like crazy. There were marigolds scattered among the vegetables, to keep bugs away.

"Good timing." Angie smiled and pulled off her gardening gloves. "I'm about beat and I'd love a glass of sweet tea."

"Sounds good to me."

Her mom squinted and gave her a careful look. "What's wrong?"

How many times in her life had Sophie heard those words? Thousands? Up to a certain point in her life she'd always shared. And then she'd stopped sharing because everything became public knowledge in the Cooper house. Jackson had found her poetry and read it on the school bus. Mia had found a love letter to a boy and read it at dinner. She'd shared a secret with Heather and of course Heather couldn't wait to get home and tell.

Looking back, it all seemed silly. Those were the things that happened in families. But in a family the size of hers, they happened with more frequency. She'd become a little too guarded. She could admit that now.

As an adult it was easier to see where she'd made mistakes, the wrong paths she'd taken. She'd also fought too hard to be independent because she'd always had her dad or brothers stepping in to take care of things for her.

Keeton had never been that way. He'd never taken over. Once he realized she could do something on her own, he let her do it. In the past few weeks he'd continued that habit. She could see that now. She should have seen it sooner.

But he had a point. Would she always compare him to Kade? Would he become a replacement for the person she lost?

"Soph?" Her mom reached for her hand. "Let's have tea."

Sophie walked with her mom to the backyard and through the back patio door into the big kitchen with the giant-size table that now had to be added to in order to make room for the sons-and daughters-in-law that had joined the family, as well as grandchildren. For now they used fold-up tables when everyone got together.

"Sit." Angie Cooper pointed at the table. "I'll get the tea."

"Mom, I can get my own tea."

"I want to get it." Her mom filled two glasses

with ice and then pulled a glass pitcher out of the fridge. "Lemon?"

"No."

And then they were sitting across from each other, and her mom was waiting. Sophie sipped her tea and tried to tell herself that it was crazy to be afraid. After all of these years, why keep hiding things?

"Mom, about Kade…" She closed her eyes and felt her mom's hand on hers. "Have you heard from Reese lately?"

"Don't change the subject."

Sophie opened her eyes and smiled. "I've been thinking about him a lot lately."

"Having Keeton back in town probably hasn't helped. I think you always kind of had a crush on him, didn't you?"

"I meant Reese. I've been thinking of Reese." Her little brother had joined the military and was in Afghanistan.

"Oh." Angie Cooper swirled her glass. "Pray for your brother. He's being sent somewhere. He said he can't talk too much right now but he'll call in a few weeks."

"I wish he'd stayed home where he belongs."

Angie Cooper nodded and her hand continued to cover Sophie's. "Honey, there's something we learn in life. We can pray hard but we can't always protect the people we love. We can't make the decisions for them. Now why don't you tell me what's going on?"

"It's what went on. Mom, Kade and I…"

"I know."

"You knew?" Heat crawled up Sophie's cheeks. "How?"

"A mother knows these things. I guess I should have talked to you about it. But then we lost Kade and…and I guess I thought it would only hurt more if we talked."

"Mom, I was pregnant. When Kade died, I was pregnant."

Sophie's eyes warmed but she didn't cry. She was all cried out.

"Oh, Sophie, why didn't you come to me?"

"I was embarrassed."

"Embarrassed? I'm sure you were heartbroken and afraid. I'm so sorry you didn't feel like you could talk to me."

"I'm sorry that I didn't." Sophie sipped her tea and after a few minutes returned to the conversation. "I didn't know how to tell you. And then I miscarried."

Her mom wiped a stray tear that slid down her cheek. "It breaks my heart that I wasn't there for you. It's too late to tell you that you could have come to me."

"I know I could have, but at the time I was ashamed and I didn't want to disappoint you."

"You've never disappointed me."

"I wanted that baby. I know what we did was wrong, but losing that baby felt like losing Kade again."

"Of course you wanted it. Whatever the circumstances, the baby was still a part of you, still a baby." Her mom shook her head. "I wish I could have been there for you."

Sophie hugged her mom, and her heart felt lighter than it had in years. "I should have let you in. I'm sorry."

Her mom wiped at her eyes as Sophie sat down. "I know we're talking about the past. But, Sophie, the present is what we're living now."

"Yes, I know."

"So maybe we should still have a mother-daughter talk and you should tell me what is going on between you and Keeton."

Heat climbed up Sophie's cheeks. Way to make her feel sixteen and not thirty-five. "Well, not that, if that's what you're wondering."

Her mom laughed. "No, I wasn't really asking you about that. I wondered if you still had feelings for him."

Sophie stood. She carried her glass to the sink. Outside the kitchen window the swimming pool glimmered in late-afternoon sunlight. In the field a newborn calf followed behind its mother. She was having trouble processing the question.

"Still?"

"Sophie, you've always cared about him. I think you had a crush on him years ago, probably before you started dating Kade."

"I don't know how I feel. I know what I used to feel." She smiled as she watched the calf get close and duck under the mother's belly to nurse. "I felt guilty."

"For loving him?"

"I loved Kade." She turned to look at her mom. "I loved him from the time we were little kids on the bus together."

"And you loved him because it was easy to love him. But I'm not sure you would have married him."

Sophie turned her attention back to the calf. "Maybe not. But I don't think I loved Keeton."

"Keeton and Kade were definitely not one and the same." Her mom smiled at a memory that softened her expression. She joined Sophie at the window. "But Keeton is the man who is strong enough for you now. I think maybe you knew that then, which is another reason you felt guilty."

"I can't do this." Sophie turned on the faucet and splashed her face with water. "I wish it wasn't so hard. Keeton left. When I needed him he was gone. And now he's off riding bulls again."

"And you're mad at him, and worried about him." Angie touched her shoulder. "Right?"

"I'm something."

"It's okay to love him. Let him into your life."

It sounded so easy. Open her heart. Open her life. Let him in.

She thought about him riding bulls and she shook her head. She couldn't lose him all over again. He had a dream to chase. She wouldn't stop him because she knew how much it meant to him, but she didn't know how to love him while he was putting his life in danger.

Keeton watched the bulls go through the pen and into the chutes. The Tulsa event had always been one of his favorites. The crowds were big. The money bigger. The bulls were the meanest. Yeah, he loved Tulsa. Or he had ten years ago.

Now he hated the idea that his knee would probably give up the ghost at any minute and he had drawn a bull that never brought a good score to his rider but always managed to get him in the dirt.

To top things off, he'd allowed Becka to take Lucy for the day. The two of them were in the stands together. Actually, three of them. Becka, Lucy and Becka's new man. They'd gotten married a couple of weeks ago. Fortunately the two were going out of country. And they weren't taking his daughter with them.

He rubbed rosin on his rope in preparation for the ride to come. He thought about Sophie at home. He thought about his land, the twenty acres he'd gotten back and the two hundred he couldn't buy back. And the one hundred acres of it that Sophie had bought. Yeah, life had a way of changing a guy's plans.

"You about ready to ride?"

He turned. Jackson Cooper stood next to him, his hat low over his eyes and his lips turned in a definite frown.

"About ready." Keeton did a few stretches. At his age a guy couldn't loosen up too much. He stretched for a left leg lunge, felt his knee give. He reached for the fence to pull himself back up.

"Yeah, you look ready." Jackson shook his head. "Why are you doing this? You've got a sweet deal with Jeremy. You've got a pretty baby girl in the stands and my sister waiting for you in Dawson."

Right, he had it all. He rubbed a hand across his jaw and thought that what he really had was a bad headache and no desire to get on a bull. That didn't make sense at all.

Nothing made sense. "Thanks a lot."

He jerked off his gloves, unbuckled his chaps and tossed his bull rope at Jackson.

Jackson grinned. "You don't sound like you mean that thank-you. A guy tries to help you out a little and you act like you might rip his head off."

"I don't think you're trying to help. I think you're trying to keep things interesting for you."

Jackson's smile faded. "Well, I have to admit, life on the farm gets kind of quiet sometimes, Keet. But I'll tell you this, no one wants you to make the right decision more than I do. I spent too many nights listening to my sister cry herself to sleep in the room next to mine. And I have a bad feeling she's crying herself to sleep again."

"Again, thank you." He didn't know if he meant it or not. Maybe a little of both. "I'm withdrawing. See you later."

"You can't head home right now."

"Why not?"

"Bad accident. The road is closed."

Keeton shook his head in disbelief. "How would you know that?"

"Heard some of the guys talking about it. They heard it on the radio as they were getting here."

"You could have told me that before."

Jackson shrugged one shoulder. "Didn't think you'd do something crazy like withdrawing. So, do you want your gear back?"

Keeton took a step and shook his head. "No,

I think I'm going to talk to Doc about a long-overdue knee surgery."

And tomorrow morning, as soon as the road was open, he'd be heading back to Dawson and back to Sophie.

Chapter Sixteen

Sunlight glimmered on dew-covered fields as Sophie got into her car and headed for work. First she planned on stopping by the development to see how the houses were progressing. The Tillers were excited. She'd seen them the previous day after leaving her mom's. The walls were up on the house, windows were being put in. It was just a shell of what it would become, but it looked a lot like a house and, to a couple who'd been living in a two-bedroom apartment with their three kids, that shell of a house meant everything.

The help of neighbors meant everything. The house would cost the families in the development a fraction of normal cost because they were donating free labor to each other. What added to the huge blessing was that people in the community had learned of the project and were dropping by to help out.

People, helping people. A few contractors had even donated leftover building materials from homes they had finished.

Sophie pulled up the driveway just as the sun broke over the eastern horizon. She parked and got out. Gabe's truck was already parked near the Tillers' house. He was the only one there. She shivered and an uneasy twist to her stomach reminded her that she shouldn't be here alone.

What if Gabe's aunt and uncle were right? Maybe she should have let Keeton do something, talk to him, call the police, something. Instead she wanted to handle everything herself.

She regretted her stubbornness now.

She walked around the house, trying to let go of her unease, trying to focus on the house and the long way they'd come since starting this project. A thumping sound in the woods drew her attention from the house to the line of trees at the edge of the property.

Where was Gabe? She started to call for him and then she didn't. If he wasn't right here, there had to be a reason. She pulled her cell phone from her purse and shoved it in her pocket. If Gabe wouldn't come out of hiding, she'd go find him.

As she walked toward the tree line and the edge of the property she knew that this had to be the worst idea ever. If she saw a woman doing something like this she'd probably call her every kind of fool.

The still-small voice telling her to stop suddenly became a loud voice telling her to pay attention and let the police handle this. She stopped but it was too late. Ahead of her in the woods she saw him move. She saw the fifty-gallon barrels scattered among the trees.

For months she'd owned this property and she hadn't walked down here since that first week that it had become hers, back in late winter. She hadn't been down here since spring arrived.

The sun heated her back as she stood there watching Gabe walk around the barrels. She was several-hundred-feet away, but it looked as though he was watering plants growing in the barrels. He turned, saw her and he walked out of the woods, shielding his eyes to get a better look.

"What are you doing here?" he shouted.

"Came to check on the houses. What are you doing?" She forced her voice to sound steady, as if she hadn't noticed the barrels.

He laughed. "Right, we're going to play stupid."

With that he headed her way. Sophie backed up but she thought if she kept him engaged in conversation, maybe he would calm down. He didn't look like a man about to calm down. He looked edgy and desperate.

"I thought this might be about the land." She eased into the conversation. "You know I offered your aunt and uncle part of this land after I bought it. I didn't want to run them off their property. They decided they were too tired to keep farming."

"Yeah, and they didn't think about me, the nephew they always promised would get his share. My uncle bought that land off my granddad before my dad could scrape up the money for an acre of it."

"I'm sorry about that. I didn't know." She'd always wondered what caused a person to go over the edge. What pushed a person to do something crazy? Now she thought she knew—it was a combination. Greed. Anger. Desperation.

He had all three and then some.

"I'm going to ask you to get your stuff and get off this property, Gabe."

"I think I'm not going to do that because as soon as I do, you'll call the cops and tell them what you saw. I need those plants. If I'm ever going to have anything of my own, I need a good harvest."

"Did you burn my barn and the houses here?"

"Yeah, but not Keeton's old house. Kids did that." He was about fifty feet from her. She had a limited opportunity to run because she could see in his eyes that he wasn't going to calm down and let her walk away.

She kept backing away from him. As she walked she kicked off the high heels she'd put on for her job at the head office for Cooper Investments. She kept babbling stupid stuff about being able to help him, maybe get him a loan.

Every survival show she'd ever seen played through her mind as she finally turned and ran. Always run, the experts said. Don't stay to be a victim. Run. Even if they have a gun, running is safer than being taken somewhere.

As she ran she could hear his feet pounding behind her, getting closer. She reached into her pocket for her phone to dial 911. The operator answered, asked her what her emergency was. Sophie gave the address first and then told them she was being attacked by Gabe Gordon. She needed help.

Her brothers would hear. They would have their scanner on. Someone would get to her. But Gabe got to her first. As she reached for her car door, he pulled her back and slammed his fist across her face.

Fight.

She spun, hitting him with her elbow, and then she brought her knee up and connected. As he fell to the ground she got in her car and locked the doors. She started the car and he got to his feet and reached for her door. She shifted into reverse and hit the gas. She still had her phone and 911 was locked in. She heard the operator asking if she was still there.

"I'm here. I'm heading to town. I can't stay here alone."

In her rearview mirror she saw his truck coming after her. Sophie hit the gas and gravel flew. One thing about being a country girl, she knew how to handle a car on back roads. She peeled out of the gravel drive and onto the paved road. A half mile and she turned toward Dawson.

The truck behind her zoomed. Ahead of her she could see town. Behind her, Gabe's face twisted in anger. She took her eyes off the rearview mirror and felt a hard bump as he rammed her car. She held tight to the steering wheel trying to keep the car on the road.

In the distance she heard sirens. She said a quiet thank-you. The truck hit her again. The car spun and then tilted and slid. Glass shattered and metal crunched as her car hit the ditch and landed with a heavy thud against a tree. Sophie leaned into the steering wheel and breathed deep, past pain in her arm, past fear.

The door jerked open. She screamed and then she saw her half brother Jeremy and a police officer. She sobbed into her brother's shoulder. His hand rubbed the back of her head. He told her everything would be okay, they were taking Gabe into custody.

"He's growing marijuana," she whispered as the world tilted uncertainly and went black.

Things didn't work out the way Keeton wanted. He got stuck with Becka, working out her next visit with their daughter, which meant he didn't leave Tulsa until early Monday. But leaving was all he wanted to do. He had things he needed to tell Sophie.

Over the weekend he'd done a lot of thinking. He'd thought about walking away, about giving up the land in Dawson and staying in his house in Broken Arrow. He had enough land to raise a few head of cattle and some good horses. He could stop traveling and be a full-time dad to Lucy.

It had all felt like a pretty good plan, but every time he thought about giving up, he thought about Sophie and walking away years ago. He hadn't wanted to be Kade's replacement. As he packed the suitcase he'd dropped onto his bed, he thought about that decision all of those years ago.

He'd known back then that Sophie meant more to him than that moment they'd shared. She'd been at the back of his mind all of these years while he'd been chasing dreams and getting older. And all of that time he'd been telling himself that Sophie loved Kade and he didn't intend on being the replacement West who took her to the altar.

He'd decided last night that he wasn't a replacement. And whatever it took, he would convince her to give him a chance to be a better man than he'd ever been in his life.

Lucy. He looked at his little girl squirming around on his bed, trying like everything to grab hold of a stuffed horse rattle he'd bought. It was just out of her reach and she was scooting, trying to get it. As he watched she flipped her left leg over her right, reached with her left hand—and over she went.

"Hey, kiddo, you rolled over." He reached to pick her up and she grinned as if she had a real idea of what she'd done.

"We need to go home and show Sophie." Because lately when he thought of himself and Lucy, Sophie was always in the picture. She completed their family.

And after all of these years, he thought a bigger family might be exactly what he wanted.

The phone rang. He reached for it, distracted by Lucy pushing fingers in his mouth. "Hello."

"Hey, it's Jackson. We need to head back to Dawson."

"Do what? Why we? Don't you have a load of bulls to take home?"

"Keet, Sophie's been in an accident. They've arrested Gabe, and she's in the hospital."

Keeton eased his baby girl's fingers out of his mouth and sat down on the edge of the bed. "What happened?"

"She caught Gabe in the middle of tending some plants he had in barrels on the edge of that land."

"That's why he wanted her gone. She should have let me call the police."

Silence hung between them for a few seconds. Jackson finally spoke. "What do you mean? You knew?"

"No, but his aunt and uncle stopped by to warn her that they thought it might be Gabe."

"And she didn't tell. It's about time she stopped keeping everything to herself, like telling the family will take away her freedom."

"Yeah, she does have an issue with that." Keeton stood and reached for his suitcase. "Do you want a ride or do you have a truck there?"

"Travis is going to bring the livestock home. I'll ride with you."

"Gotcha." He walked out the back door into his garage and flung the suitcase into the bed of the truck. "Jackson, is she okay?"

"She's stable. Light concussion and a broken arm."

Keeton exhaled and kissed his daughter on

the cheek. He stuck her in the car seat before responding. "I'll be at the arena as quick as I can get there from my place."

"I'll be waiting."

As Keeton drove down his driveway he saw that the realtor had already put up a sign. He guessed he should have sold this place first, then he wouldn't have been tempted to come back. But he'd wanted a place to go if things in Dawson didn't work out.

He hadn't planned on Sophie when he went home. He'd thought about seeing her. He'd smiled over the past. He'd never thought about what he'd felt and wondered if those feelings had changed. Back then he'd been a kid, really. Now he knew what he wanted.

It didn't take long to get to the arena. When Jackson climbed in the passenger side, Keeton ignored the look the other man gave him. He shifted gears and headed for home. For Dawson.

"You okay to drive?" Jackson finally asked as they were heading down the highway.

"Yeah, I'm good."

"Are you planning to marry my sister?" Jackson reclined his seat a little. He glanced in the back seat of the crew cab truck and made goofy noises at Lucy. She started to cry.

Keeton smiled and laughed a little at his

daughter's very discerning taste. "Smart girl, my daughter."

"I'll bring her around. Babies love me."

"Right."

"About my sister?"

"I'm not talking to you about my plans until I talk to Sophie."

"I'll take that as a yes."

Keeton kept driving. They were nearly to Grove. Jackson had somehow managed to fall asleep. Keeton relaxed a little. And he prayed a lot. He had a box in the glove compartment of his truck. He had memorized all of the right words, even though he couldn't think of them now. Yeah, he planned on marrying Sophie Cooper.

If she'd say yes. And he had to admit to a few doubts. Worse than doubts, he had a bad case of nerves. By the time he pulled into the hospital parking lot he felt as though he might have a bad stomach virus.

He reached for the antacid he kept in the console between the seats. Jackson woke up. He grinned at Keeton as Keeton popped two tablets in his mouth.

"Got a case of nerves?"

Keeton swigged from a bottle of water. "No, I'm fine."

Jackson laughed and reached for the door handle. "I've seen you calmer than a summer day getting on some of the meanest, baddest bulls in the business. I've never seen you look this green."

"Yeah, yeah, whatever." He pulled a thin, paper bag out of the console as he put the antacids back in.

"What's that?"

Keeton ignored him and reached in for the box.

"Wow, you've got this all planned out. No spur-of-the-moment for you."

"A guy has to do what a guy has to do."

"What's in the envelope?" Jackson reached but Keeton pulled back.

"Cards."

"Cards? Plural?"

"Could you stop asking questions? We need to check on Sophie."

Jackson got out of the truck and reached in the back for Lucy. "Tell you what, Romeo, why don't you head on in there and I'll find the family and ask them how she's doing."

"They're probably in her room."

Jackson shrugged and pulled his phone out of his pocket. "They're about to vacate her room. Go make my sister a happy woman."

Keeton tipped his hat and headed for the hospital. He glanced back once. Jackson was holding Lucy, talking in the phone and grinning.

As Keeton walked through the doors of the hospital he prayed that God would make things right and that Sophie would give him a chance to be the man who would stay in her life.

Chapter Seventeen

Sophie woke up in the shadowy room where they'd taken her after the initial exam in the E.R. They had promised she could go home later, maybe early evening. She hoped so. A hospital bed and hospital food weren't in her plans.

But then, getting run off the road by Gabe hadn't been in her plans, either. She'd been awake and watched as the police shoved him into the back of a patrol car back at the scene of the accident. She never would have guessed Gabe, not in a million years.

"You okay, Soph?"

She turned, smiled at her mom and nodded. "I'm good. How about you?"

Angie smiled. "Better now that I know you're okay."

"It's a broken arm."

"It could have been worse."

Sophie nodded and tears burned behind her eyelids. She moved and the cast on her left arm felt heavy and hot. "Great way to spend the summer."

"Why didn't you call someone?" Her mom's worried voice took Sophie's attention off the cast, the headache, the regrets.

"I thought I could handle it."

"Without getting everyone involved."

Ouch. Sophie reached to push the button that would raise her head so she could see her mom a little better. "I think I've learned my lesson. There are definitely times to let my family be involved."

"That's good to know." Her dad stood in the doorway, his blond hair touched with gray but he still stood straight and tall. She smiled at him.

"Yeah, we learn from our mistakes." She sighed and looked up at the ceiling, wondering if God had heard all of her apologies, her regrets, her pleading just hours earlier.

"Mom and I need to step out for a few minutes. Is there anything we can get you while we're gone?" Her dad shot a smile at her mom that Sophie didn't miss. And then he winked.

Sophie's mom stood and joined him at the door, looking a little narrow-eyed and perplexed by her husband's sudden appearance and insistence that they needed to leave.

"I'm good. If you wanted to, you could shoot

me back in time and help me make some better decisions."

"I think you've made good decisions, just sometimes a little late in the game."

"Right, but at my age, that isn't really a home run."

He laughed and hooked an arm through her mom's. "You'll make it. We'll be back."

Sophie nodded and closed her eyes. She leaned back on the pillow that crinkled a little with the pressure of her head. She reached with her right arm to fluff, but it was unfluffable. She groaned and reached for the television remote.

A light rap on the door pulled her attention from a program that had originally aired in the seventies. She flicked the volume and looked at the door. "Come in."

Boot footsteps. She held her breath, hopeful, afraid, not wanting to be let down. At her age, getting rejected really wasn't a horse she could get back on.

Keeton walked in the room, carrying a brown bag, and a bouquet of slightly wilted carnations. "Surprise."

He put the flowers on the table next to the bed.

"Beautiful." She smiled at the colorful, if wilted, bouquet.

"The gift shop is low on flowers." He reached for the light but she stopped him.

"No light. I have bruises on my face, no make-up, my hair is a mess."

"You look beautiful to me." He pulled a chair close.

"Yes, because the light is off."

He didn't talk for a minute. He looked up and took a deep breath and then he shook his head. She wanted to touch his cheek. She wanted to reach for his hand. She didn't let herself do either. Not yet. Not even to wipe the worry from his expression.

"I was worried." He reached for her hand and pulled it to his lips. He held it there, and then brushed his cheek across her knuckles.

"I'm fine."

"Yes, you're fine." He held up a bag and handed it to her. "I bought you a card."

She laughed and pulled out a dozen cards. "A card?"

"Okay, more than one. I didn't know if I should pick out a get-well card, a funny card, a serious card with a big foldout picture, a poem, or a card to tell you how much I love you."

"I see." She flipped through the cards and came to a particularly cheesy one with a big flower on the front. When she opened it a butterfly popped out. "Not this one."

She opened another and it played an old love song. "Cute."

He grinned and shrugged shoulders she'd really have liked to lean into. "I liked it."

"I'd much rather just talk than read what other people have to say." She reached for his hand again. "I don't ever want you to leave again."

"Really?"

She nodded, and looked down at the hand in hers. His was much darker than her own from working outside in the sun. She sat in an office most of the time.

"I don't want to lose you."

"I don't want to lose you, either." He held her hand a little tighter. "As a matter of fact, I'm here to talk about a dream of mine. You remember, you told me to get my own dream?"

"I remember. In retrospect, that might have been kind of harsh."

"A little, but well deserved."

"What is your new dream?" She wanted to shout, *me, me, me,* but she remained quiet.

"My dream is about Lucy, who happens to be with Jackson right now. It also includes some land, most of which belongs to you. There's a house with a porch swing. Umm, also owned by you. Maybe a few mules. And more kids."

"Very sweet. Is there a wife in your dream world?"

He nodded and his eyes crinkled at the corners as his smile widened. "Oh, very much so."

"I think it's a great dream."

"I'd rather it be reality." She noticed his hands trembling as he reached into his pocket. When she saw the box in his hand, her throat tightened and she blinked fast to clear her vision.

"Keeton…"

He looked up. "Please, let me finish before you say no."

"I'm not going to say no."

He grinned again. "Well then, let me finish because I've practiced for two days and I'd hate to ruin a perfectly good proposal."

She clamped her lips tight and he reached for her hand again. "I know this is the wrong finger, we'll fix that as soon as you're able to wear a ring on your other hand. But, Sophie Cooper, I'd very much love for you to be my wife. Because I love you. If you'll have a retired bull rider who wants to take care of you and make some dreams of his own come true."

She nodded and tears ran down her cheeks. He used the corner of the sheet to brush them away and then he held her, his lips firm, his arms strong. She leaned close and wrapped her arm around his waist because she didn't want to let go. She didn't want to wake up and find that none of this had been real.

"Keeton, you aren't a dream, are you?"

Keeton laughed at the hesitation in Sophie's

voice. He touched her cheek and then buried his fingers in the hair at the nape of her neck, pulling her close to kiss her again.

"This is not a dream. Well, unless we're both dreaming the same dream. In my dream I just asked you to marry me and you said yes."

She laughed and trembled in his arms. "Yes, that's the dream I had, too. That must mean I'm conscious?"

"I think so. I love you."

"I love…" She stopped, squinting her eyes at a loud commotion in the hall.

"Excuse me, messy baby coming through." Jackson fast-walked into the room, holding Lucy out. The baby giggled.

Keeton groaned. So much for the perfect proposal, the perfect moment. He took his little girl and she gurgled at him and reached for his nose. Next to him, Sophie laughed.

Okay, maybe the moment hadn't been ruined. Maybe this made it a little more perfect.

Jackson turned a little red and backed toward the door. "I hope I didn't interrupt."

"You're not sorry and you know it," Sophie called out as her brother continued his retreat. He stopped at the door.

Keeton put Lucy on a nearby chair and reached into the bag Jackson had dropped on the floor.

The woman he planned on marrying just as soon as possible pointed at her brother.

"Come back here, right now," she ordered and Jackson obeyed. "Don't you want to see my ring?"

Jackson let out a holler and hurried back to Sophie's side. He looked as though he was about to lift her up off the bed and spin her. Keeton cleared his throat. "Don't hurt her, okay."

"Right, yeah, of course." Jackson slowed down and leaned in to hug his sister. "Congratulations. It's about time the two of you got it right."

Keeton had to agree. He'd finally gotten it right. Sophie. Lucy. Dawson. At long last his life was coming together. He sent up a prayer of thanks and had a vision of his future as part of a loving family. He had found his dream. And it was coming true.

* * * * *

Look for Brenda Minton's next
COOPER CREEK *novel*
from Love Inspired Books,
THE RANCHER'S SECRET WIFE,
available in August.

Dear Reader,

The Bull Rider's Baby wasn't supposed to be the next book in the Cooper Creek series. I had other plans. But then along came Sophie Cooper and Keeton West. Life happens that way, too. We make plans. We think we have it all figured out. We start filling God in on our plans rather than listening to His. We get sidetracked, a little distracted, we lose focus. Sometimes we lose faith.

In this book Keeton and Sophie have both been derailed by one common tragedy. They are living separate lives, going in different directions. When their paths cross again they learn that God has a way of changing lives in unexpected ways.

Brenda Minton

Questions for Discussion

1. At the convenience store, Keeton West hides from Sophie. Why? Would you have done the same? Why or why not?

2. Sophie is afraid of her emotions when she sees Keeton. What causes that fear? The past? Or what she feels now?

3. Keeton is back in Dawson with a lot of plans for reclaiming what was once his. Is it really possible to go home again? What changes when a person tries to reclaim the past?

4. Sophie is hiding the fact that she is building the houses on the land across from Keeton. Why would she want to keep that a secret?

5. Why is Sophie adamant about keeping things from her family? Is it about hiding something or about independence?

6. Sophie is unsure of her feelings for Keeton. She loved his brother. She has feelings for Keeton. Is her insight correct, that what she and Kade shared might have changed as they matured?

7. Keeton is determined to win a world title in bull riding because it was his brother's dream. How is this a good idea, how is it bad?

8. Keeton's parents reacted to Kade's death by moving away from everything and everyone they knew. Sometimes we react to pain and make wrong choices. What would you have done?

9. Keeton is falling in love with Sophie. Or maybe he always loved her. But he pushed her away because he didn't want her to always compare him to his brother, and he didn't want to wonder if he was a replacement. Is his thinking logical? Was time and distance the best thing for them after Kade's death?

10. Keeton tells Sophie to trust that God will keep him safe. Why is that so difficult when facing a fear? Like Sophie's fear of watching bull riding, or dating a bull rider.

11. What does Sophie's family learn about giving Sophie space to be her own person? How does simple communication play into these relationships?

12. Keeton is willing to give Sophie space, even though he loves her and wants her in his life. What changes her feelings for him?

LARGER-PRINT BOOKS!

GET 2 FREE LARGER-PRINT NOVELS PLUS 2 FREE MYSTERY GIFTS

Love Inspired

Larger-print novels are now available...

YES! Please send me 2 FREE LARGER-PRINT Love Inspired® novels and my 2 FREE mystery gifts (gifts are worth about $10). After receiving them, if I don't wish to receive any more books, I can return the shipping statement marked "cancel". If I don't cancel, I will receive 6 brand-new novels every month and be billed just $4.99 per book in the U.S. or $5.49 per book in Canada. That's a saving of at least 23% off the cover price. It's quite a bargain! Shipping and handling is just 50¢ per book in the U.S. and 75¢ per book in Canada.* I understand that accepting the 2 free books and gifts places me under no obligation to buy anything. I can always return a shipment and cancel at any time. Even if I never buy another book, the two free books and gifts are mine to keep forever.

122/322 IDN FEG3

Name	(PLEASE PRINT)	
Address		Apt. #
City	State/Prov.	Zip/Postal Code

Signature (if under 18, a parent or guardian must sign)

Mail to the Reader Service:
IN U.S.A.: P.O. Box 1867, Buffalo, NY 14240-1867
IN CANADA: P.O. Box 609, Fort Erie, Ontario L2A 5X3

Not valid to current subscribers to Love Inspired Larger-Print books.

Are you a current subscriber to Love Inspired books and want to receive the larger-print edition? Call 1-800-873-8635 or visit www.ReaderService.com.

* Terms and prices subject to change without notice. Prices do not include applicable taxes. Sales tax applicable in N.Y. Canadian residents will be charged applicable taxes. Offer not valid in Quebec. This offer is limited to one order per household. All orders subject to credit approval. Credit or debit balances in a customer's account(s) may be offset by any other outstanding balance owed by or to the customer. Please allow 4 to 6 weeks for delivery. Offer available while quantities last.

Your Privacy—The Reader Service is committed to protecting your privacy. Our Privacy Policy is available online at www.ReaderService.com or upon request from the Reader Service.

We make a portion of our mailing list available to reputable third parties that offer products we believe may interest you. If you prefer that we not exchange your name with third parties, or if you wish to clarify or modify your communication preferences, please visit us at www.ReaderService.com/consumerchoice or write to us at Reader Service Preference Service, P.O. Box 9062, Buffalo, NY 14269. Include your complete name and address.

LILP11B